RON ORLIS

AND THE
JAMES BAY
ADVENTURE

RON ORLIS AND THE JAMES BAY ADVENTURE

BERNARD PALMER

Please note that several books in the Danny Orlis series are published by Sword of the Lord Publications and are available for purchase on their website, www.swordbooks.com.

Aneko Press Youth

www.anekopress.com

Aneko Press, Life Sentence Publishing, and our logos are trademarks of Life Sentence Publishing, Inc.
203 E. Birch Street
P.O. Box 652
Abbotsford, WI 54405

JUVENILE FICTION / Religious / Christian / Action & Adventure
Paperback ISBN: 979-8-88936-008-7
eBook ISBN: 979-8-88936-009-4
10 9 8 7 6 5 4 3 2 1
Available where books are sold

CONTENTS

CHAPTER 1

CAPTAIN RON ORLIS

It was spring at Cedarton Bible Institute in northern Minnesota. The last snow had melted, the ice was gone, and the grass was as green as the tiny new leaves that were coming out to cloak the poplar, birch, and oak. However, the students on the Bible school campus were far too busy to enjoy the gentle caress of the warming sun or the whispering of the wind. There were term papers to write, Scripture to memorize, and finals to cram for. The library was crowded and the social rooms all but deserted during this last surge of activity before the school year ended.

Ron Orlis would have been studying, too, except for the fact that Danny had flown in unexpectedly and insisted on having dinner with him.

"I know this is a bad time," Danny said on his phone, "but I'll promise not to keep you out too late."

"As a matter of fact, I'm not in too bad shape as

far as studying goes," Ron told him. "My term papers are in, and I don't have my first final until the end of next week."

"I'll borrow Mr. Forester's car and be out in half an hour."

Ron was waiting for him on the dormitory steps.

"Well, Danny, just what is this visit all about?" Ron asked, getting into the car.

"Can't I come and visit you without having a special reason?"

"Sure, you can, but you never have."

"Now that's no way to talk to your big brother." Danny pulled up before a little, out-of-the-way cafe and stopped. "Have you got any plans for this summer, Ron?"

"Nothing definite. I had planned on going to some Bible camp to work as a counselor, but I must have decided a little late, or something. At least, nothing has opened up."

"Praise the Lord for that."

Ron's forehead wrinkled quizzically.

"What do you mean, Danny? Have you got something for me?"

"That's what I came to talk with you about."

The waitress came and took their orders.

"Do you remember my telling you that the Mission bought the buildings the Hudson Bay Company abandoned when they closed down their installation at Old Factory?" Danny Orlis continued.

"That's been some time ago, hasn't it?"

"That's right." He picked up his fork and toyed with it absent-mindedly. "We got the buildings for a ridiculously low price, providing we got them torn down and moved within a specified time. Now time's about to run out. We have to get them moved this summer or lose them."

"I see. And you want me to come up and help tear them down. Is that it?"

"Not exactly. We need somebody to run the boat, hauling lumber from Old Factory up to Paint Hills and the other places where we're planning to open mission stations."

Ron's eyes widened.

"You're joking."

"I'm serious, Ron," Danny countered. "The original plan was for me to go up and run the *Good News* for them, but there's so much flying to be done that the Board feels I can't be spared. They had a meeting last night and asked me to come over today and talk to you."

"B-b-but I don't know anything about James Bay," he spluttered. "And I don't know very much about running a boat like the *Good News* or whatever her name is."

"You've had a summer's experience with Cap on the Lake of the Woods, so you've handled a schooner in rough water. You know how to read a compass, take bearings, and plot a course."

"I don't know anything about running a boat in tides, Danny," he persisted. "And I don't know anything about James Bay. I wouldn't know where the reefs and sandbars are, or anything."

"Jay Russell will be helping you, Ron. He is a veteran missionary in the area and knows the people and the language, even though he's had no experience on boats. And we've hired Charlie Eneveloe, an Indian pilot who knows the east side of James Bay the way you and I know the Angle in the Lake of the Woods."

Ron Orlis leaned forward, his lean young face serious.

"Tell me honestly, Danny, do you think I can handle the job?"

"If I didn't, Ron, I wouldn't even be here." He was silent for almost a minute. "I'd forgotten to tell you that this will be an evangelistic effort, too. One of our Indian evangelists, Frank Thomas, will be going along to do visitation and hold services wherever possible."

Ron Orlis picked up his water glass, drank slowly, and returned it to the table.

"You make it awfully hard for me to turn you down."

"I don't mean to," Danny answered. "We want the Lord's will in this matter."

"I've been praying that God would lead me into whatever He wants me to do this summer, but nothing has opened up. Now this comes along. There's a real need and it's something you seem to think I can do. It looks to me that we have the Lord's will."

Danny's eyes lit.

"We all felt that way at Board meeting last night."

* * *

Ron Orlis took his final exams at CBI and went home to the Angle to spend the few days waiting for word to come that the ice had gone out on James Bay. The day after the message came through, Danny flew up to Angle Inlet, picked up Ron, and went on up to The Pass north of Winnipeg to get the Indian evangelist. Shortly after noon the next day they settled down on the runway at Moose Factory on the southern tip of James Bay.

Ron got out of the plane and looked about, but there was no one there. Disappointment gleamed in his eyes.

"I thought Mr. Russell and the Indian pilot would be waiting for us, Danny," he said. "Did they know when we were to be here?"

"They wired us that they would be here when we got here. They may be up at the Bradshaws. They're the missionaries for this area. Or something may have come up to delay them."

They went over to the mission home in Moose Factory and found out that Jay Russell had sent a message to them over the two-way radio system that linked the mission stations.

"Jay said to tell you that they are fogbound," Mr. Bradshaw said genially, "but would be here as soon as the fog lifts so they can get into the air. In the meantime, you're to stay with us."

Ron and the others tried to prevail upon Danny Orlis to stay until the following morning, but he insisted on going back as soon as he had refueled.

"There's so much flying to do these next three or four months," he said, "that I can't afford to waste even half a day."

When Danny was gone, Ron turned to Frank Thomas.

"Let's go down and take a look at the boat we'll be living on this summer."

They walked along the dusty road through the short business district of the weather-beaten little community, down to the shore of James Bay. Shading his eyes against the brilliant northern sun, he stared out across the ice-blue water.

"We've got a big job this summer, Frank," Ron said at last. "James Bay looks treacherous to me."

"It is." The Indian spoke cryptically. Then his voice softened. "But that's not what I see when I look out there. I see the hundreds of Indians who live in isolated villages on the shores of the Bay who have never heard the good news that the Lord Jesus Christ can save them from sin."

Ron turned to read the love and longing for his lost people in Frank Thomas's eyes. In that moment, a bond formed between the two of them.

"Where did Mr. Bradshaw say the *Good News* is?" the Orlis boy asked at last.

"Over near the dock." Frank gestured to their

left. "There she is, still on her cradle where she was put for the winter."

They walked over to the stub-nosed little schooner and examined her.

"She doesn't look very big, does she, when you think of taking her out on a body of water the size of the Bay?" Ron asked.

"A good sturdy hull," the Indian evangelist said. "Oak. She is a strong boat, Ron. She will do."

Frank had climbed aboard, and the young American was about to do the same when a voice stopped him.

"Hello there, Mister."

Startled, Ron turned to see a bony, thin-faced Indian lad of 13 or 14 standing before him. The boy was wearing a pair of old moccasins, tattered jeans, and a shirt with one button. His shirt front gaped open above and below, exposing long expanses of skin. Dirt was ground into his hands and neck and face, and black hair bushed over his ears.

He eyed Ron, a smile crinkling his homely face appealingly.

"How are you?"

"Is this your boat, Mister?"

"Not exactly."

"Are you the captain?" he persisted hopefully. "Are you going to be shipping out on her?"

"I guess you might say that. At least I'll be responsible for her. Let's put it that way."

The boy drew himself up to his full height.

"My name is Eddie Skeena."

"My name is Ron Orlis. You can call me Ron."

There was a moment's hesitation.

"Do–do you need a 'hand' on your boat this summer, Mister?"

The Orlis boy stifled a smile, Eddie Skeena was as slender as a birch sapling and small for his age.

"You're not very big for a 'hand,' are you?"

"I am good and strong." He flexed his puny muscles confidently. "See. I can lift anchor. I can load boat. I can unload boat. I be good hand."

"Why do you want to go out on the *Good News*, Eddie?" he asked. "How come you don't want to stay home anymore?"

"My home at Fort George," the boy said, his eyes gleaming. "That what I want to do. I want to go home."

"And why are you way down here?"

"Come down to hospital," the boy said quickly.

"Now Eddie Skeena well – want to go home."

Ron leaned against the hull of the *Good News* and smiled down at the boy.

"I can't make you any promises about taking you along, Eddie. I'm afraid we're going to be heavily loaded. And besides, we won't be at Fort George for quite a while. But I'll talk to Mr. Bradshaw. He'll know what to do about getting you back home."

The hurt leaped to the boy's face.

"I be good hand, Mister R-Ron."

"You come with me to the Bradshaw's. We'll get you back to Fort George some way."

"You change your mind, I see you." Eddie Skeena turned. "I make good 'hand.'" With that he was gone.

Ron and Frank Thomas asked Harry Bradshaw about him when they got back to the missionary's house later that afternoon.

"I wouldn't worry about him if I were you. If the government brought him down here to school or to the hospital, they'll see that he gets back."

"Hasn't the government supply boat gone up the coast yet?" his wife asked.

"Not yet. And I don't have any idea when it will be going. But I'll do some inquiring around about this boy. I'll find out where he lives and make arrangements for him to get home on the government supply boat whenever it goes."

The following day at about noon, Jay Russell and Charlie Eneveloe were flown into Moose Factory by the mission plane that was stationed on the Bay's east coast. The missionary had his 14-year-old son with him.

"Ron and Frank," Jay said, "this is my boy, Tip. He came along to help out however he can."

"Fine." Ron took Tip Russell's hand warmly. "Glad to know you, Tip."

At the dinner table that evening they made plans for getting the *Good News* into the water and loaded with gasoline and supplies.

"I've already made arrangements for a 'cat' to push

her out on the mud flats at low tide," Mr. Bradshaw said. "Then, when the tide comes in, she'll float off the cradle and be ready to go."

"Sounds simple," Ron said.

"It's not very complicated to get her into the water," Jay put in. "Then we've got to get her checked out and loaded. We should be able to start up to Old Factory in a couple of days if everything goes well."

Early the next morning as the tide ran out, Ron Orlis and the others clustered about the *Good News*, shivering in the stiff, on-shore wind.

"I'm glad we're not putting out in this weather," Ron said.

Jay Russell laughed.

"When we've been on the Bay a while, you'll think this is a beautiful day."

They skidded the *Good News* out on the mud flats and securely anchored her. While waiting for the tide to come in they hauled barrels of gasoline down on the dock and started to haul supplies. The tide came in and the *Good News* was floated off her cradle. Charlie Eneveloe and Ron Orlis took her out to the dock where the job of loading her began. Stopping only to eat, they worked late at night until the last barrel of gas and flour was aboard. Toward late afternoon Eddie Skeena came down to the dock and sat dolefully on one of the pilings, his somber eyes staring fixedly at Ron. But he did not come over to him or answer his wave.

"Makes me feel like a heel to see him sitting there that way," Ron said, "and to know that I can't help him."

Tip came over to where the Orlis boy was standing.

"I hope that's the end of the loading," he said wearily. "I tell you, I'm bushed."

"You aren't alone."

"It'll be good to get out on the water so we can get some rest."

"If that wind doesn't go down, there won't be any rest," Ron told him.

When they finished the loading, they tied the *Good News* to the dock and left Charlie Eneveloe on board to serve as guard and to keep the bilge pump operating every 30 minutes to keep the water seepage down to safe levels. After a few days the thick oak planking would be tight and require only occasional pumping in heavy seas, but now the task was a regular one.

The wind had gone down during the night, Ron noted gratefully early the next morning. Ground swells would be running and there would be some choppiness, but the big blow he had feared did not materialize.

Ron glanced at his watch.

"Four-thirty, Jay. Are we ready?"

"As ready as we'll ever be."

"Let's go."

Tip Russell loosened the stern line and sprang nimbly aboard while his dad loosened the bowline and did the same. Charlie Eneveloe backed the *Good*

News from the dock and brought her expertly about to take her out the channel to sea. Behind him, Ron Orlis had the map and was making the necessary computations to plot their course.

The pilot watched him doubtfully.

"You steer boat with wheel," he said, "not pencil."

The *Good News* was a sturdy boat, but a plodder. She did not race over the waves, she slogged into them, taking them full force against the prow and shaking them off like a fullback shakes off tacklers on an off-center smash.

Ron's confidence in the little schooner grew. She was, as Frank Thomas said, a good, honest boat.

Tip Russell came into the wheelhouse and watched him curiously.

"What're you doing?" he wanted to know.

"I'm plotting our course."

The boy frowned. "Can't you just find out how many degrees Old Factory is east of north and get the compass reading?" the boy asked.

"It isn't quite as simple as that," Ron told him. "If you'll look on this map you will see that the deviation of magnetic north from true north is 22 degrees. So, we have to add 22 degrees to our compass reading. Then we've got to get the direction of the wind and its velocity and figure its effect on our boat's course. Once that is done, we plot the effect of the tides – they run north-south here, and we are ready to get our compass heading."

"By the time you get all of that done, Tip, Charlie, he have boat at Old Factory," the pilot said contemptuously.

Something in Charlie's voice disturbed Ron Orlis. Although he scarcely knew him, the Indian pilot acted as though he disliked and distrusted him. When he finished plotting the course, Ron put the map away and got to his feet.

"If you think it is all right for me to take over for a while, Charlie," he said, "I'll spell you for a while."

Without comment the Indian turned the wheel over to him.

Ron Orlis checked the compass and corrected their heading by two degrees. This was going to be different than crossing the Big Traverse of the Lake of the Woods. There he had known all the compass headings by heart and made allowances for the velocity and direction of the wind almost subconsciously.

Tip Russell came up and stood beside him.

"Can I steer for a while, Ron?" he asked.

"After we get out a little farther and when the Bay is a little more calm than it is right now."

For an hour or more Tip perched in the wheelhouse talking with Ron about the good times he used to have at Angle Inlet and the fishing there. Finally, the Orlis boy turned to Tip.

"Why don't you go down in the galley and get us a couple of candy bars?"

Tip got to his feet.

"Where'll I find them?"

"In one of the cupboards on the starboard side, aft." He scurried away.

Ron checked the compass reading again. The *Good News* responded readily to a touch of the helm. He was still admiring her quick action and getting the feel of the rudder when Tip Russell bolted into the wheelhouse, mouth gaping, and his blue eyes wide with fear.

"R-R-R-Ron! Ron!"

"What's the matter?" The boy's fright kindled a similar flame in his own eyes. "What is it?"

"Ron, th-th-there's somebody down in the galley."

"Come now, Tim," Ron scoffed. "It must be your imagination."

"Th-th-th-then my imagination eats candy bars and cheese and c-c-crackers," he blurted. "I–I–I tell you, there's somebody down there, Ron! I saw him myself!"

CHAPTER 2

AN EXTRA MEMBER ABOARD

Ron Orlis took a long breath and expelled the air slowly.

"If there's anybody in there," he said, "it's got to be Charlie or Frank or your dad. They're the only ones aboard besides us."

"I–I know," Tip said, his teeth chattering. "Th-th-th-that's what s-s-scared me so when I opened the galley and–and there he was!"

Ron squinted down at him.

"Just exactly what did he look like?" he asked.

"I–I don't know for sure, but he was a great big guy and he had this big old knife and–" the missionary boy's eyes rolled and his voice broke. "Wh-what're we going to do, Ron? We–we couldn't just leave him down there until we get where we're going, c-c-could we?"

"We can't do that," Ron answered. "Go and get someone to take over the wheel for a couple of minutes,

Tip. Then you and I can go down below and see what it is that scared you so badly."

"I already know what it is! It's a man! We–we don't have to go down there to find that out."

"You go and get someone to take over here."

In half a minute the boy was back with Frank Thomas.

"Tip said you wanted to see me."

Ron grinned.

"Will you take over the wheel for a few minutes, Frank? Tip and I are going below."

"O.K. but stay out of the galley."

The boy's eyes widened incredulously.

"Wh-what do you kn-kn-know about the galley?"

"I've got a boy of my own about your age," Frank laughed. "There isn't anything he's more interested in than eating."

They left the wheelhouse and crossed to the hatch that went below.

"T-t-take it easy, Ron," Tip whispered, "This g-g-g-guy's about ten feet tall!"

They made their way to the galley and Ron Orlis reached out to open the door. Tip Russell was breathing heavily.

"M-m-m-maybe we sh-should go and get the other guys, Ron. He might be able to take you and m-m-me."

For an answer, Ron Orlis threw open the galley door. Tip Russell gasped aloud.

"Well, Tip, where is he?"

The boy stared about the galley.

"He–he was right in here," he said lamely. "Honest, I saw him."

The youthful captain of the *Good News* reached out and rumpled the boy's hair.

"Yes, Tip, I believe you, all right. I think you saw something like your shadow on the wall, or maybe the corner of a cupboard door–"

Tip Russell snorted indignantly. "I'll show you, Ron. You just wait. You'll find out that there is a guy on board – and that he was in the galley, too. He is about half a foot taller than you are and weighs about twice as much and–"

"You're going to have to quit reading those ghost stories, Tip, that's all there is to it. They'll get the best of you."

"Aren't you going to look for him anymore?"

"I thought maybe we'd better wait until midnight," Ron went on with mock sincerity. "That's when the witches and the hobgoblins prowl."

"Well," Frank said when they returned, "did you find what you went after?"

"Nope. The cupboard was bare."

When Ron turned around Tip Russell was gone. In five minutes, the boy was back.

"Ron," he said, excitement edging his voice. "How m-m-many candy bars did you say you bought?"

"Three boxes, I guess. I thought they'd come in handy."

"W-w-were they full boxes?"

"Sure. They didn't even have the seals broken."

"I asked Dad and I asked Charlie if they'd taken any and they both said no – did either of you fellows take any?"

They both shook their heads.

"And neither have I." Tip whipped a box of candy bars from behind his back and opened it triumphantly. "Look at this, will you? Four candy bars are gone!"

Ron Orlis stared at the box.

"Now, will you believe me when I tell you th-th-that there's someone on board?"

Ron Orlis frowned.

"I think you and I had better go below again, Tip."

"What's this all about?" the Indian evangelist asked.

"We'll tell you about it when we get back, Frank."

Half across the deck they met Jay Russell.

"What's all this about missing candy?" the missionary asked. "Tip, you've got Charlie and me both curious."

"He thinks he saw someone aboard who doesn't belong here," Ron said. "And now that he's shown me the candy box, I'm inclined to agree with him."

"The only thing to do is have another look," Jay said. "You go ahead, Ron, and I'll look after. If there's a stowaway aboard, it shouldn't be too much trouble to find him."

Tip Russell started with his dad but came back and went with Ron. They looked behind barrels and piles of supplies, but there was no sign of the stowaway. There wasn't even any more evidence that there had ever been a stowaway.

"No sir," Ron said at last, "unless your dad has discovered something I'm afraid we've drawn a blank."

They would have left that section of the boat, but Tip laid a hand on Ron's arm, stealthily.

"It sounded like one barrel bumping another one."

"Not the way they're tied in here," Ron retorted. "Those barrels aren't doing any bouncing around – and especially in seas like these. Oh no, that wasn't two barrels."

Ron Orlis turned back.

Back over the same ground he went, step by step, but he found nothing until he came to the barrel in the bow. Leaning forward, he peered over the rim into an up-turned face and two large, solemn dark eyes.

"Eddie Skeena!"

The Indian lad smiled uneasily.

"Hello. . . . You n-n-need a 'hand'?"

"Come out of there, Eddie, before I lose my temper!" Ron Orlis said sternly.

The boy crawled out from behind the barrel. The grin still lit his face, but the Orlis boy saw that his shoulders were trembling slightly.

"I thought I told you that we couldn't take you up to Fort George."

The young Indian had nothing to say.

Tip Russell moved up beside Ron.

"Is this the stowaway who was 10 feet tall?" the American asked.

The missionary's son swallowed hard.

"I–I think he must have been b-b-bigger than he is now wh-wh-when I saw him in the g-g-g-galley a little while ago," he blurted.

Ron directed his attention once more to their unwanted passenger.

"What do you think I should do with you?"

The smile left and Eddie's eyes widened.

"Take me to Fort George."

"We'll take you to Fort George, all right," Ron acknowledged grudgingly, "but only because it's either that or take you all the way back to Moose Factory. But you're going to have to earn your passage. I can tell you that right now. We're going to expect you to work."

When Eddie Skeena saw that nothing worse was going to happen to him, his smile returned.

"I work. You see how hard I work. I scrub the deck. I make the coffee. I keep look for rocks, I–" Words tumbled out until they could scarcely understand him.

In spite of his disgust at the Indian boy, Ron Orlis laughed.

"If you do all of that there won't be anything left for any of the rest of us to do," he said.

"You not sorry you take me by Fort George," Eddie promised him. "I be good 'hand' – best 'hand' you got!'"

"You'd better take Eddie down and show him where he'll be bunking, Tip," Ron said. "I'll go up and take the wheel from Frank and tell him what's been going on."

That evening Ron Orlis made it a point of eating at the same time Eddie did. Charlie Eneveloe was also at the table. When they finished eating Ron took the Bible from the counter behind him.

"It is our custom," he said, "to have devotions every day."

The Indian pilot's scowl deepened, but he did not put it into words.

Eddie's look was one of bewilderment.

"What you mean, 'devotions,' Ron? Never I see 'devotions.' "

Charlie pushed noisily back from the table and fire glittered in his dark eyes.

"What he means is that they want to read from the Bible and then preach to us every night for a couple of hours or so."

He stormed to his feet.

"I take boat around rocks. I find harbors. I work on engine, maybe, but I not listen to your preaching."

With that he stomped out of the galley and slammed the door so hard it rattled on the hinges. There was a brief, embarrassed silence.

"I didn't mean to offend him," Ron said. "I had no idea he was so bitter against the Bible."

"It doesn't take much to offend Charlie when it comes to the Word of God," Jay Russell said. "We use him as a pilot occasionally because there isn't another man, white, Indian or Eskimo, who knows these waters the way he does. And he works for us, even though he seems to hate us all, because he needs the money."

Tip Russell's round face grew even more serious.

"We're going to have to pray all the more for Charlie, Dad. He needs to know Christ as Savior, too."

"Of course he does," his father told him gently. "We all would like to see Charlie accept Christ as his Savior. But the thing that makes it so hard is that it has to be Charlie's decision. Neither you, nor I, nor anyone else can make it for him."

"That's the way it has to be for each of us," Ron put in. "We are each responsible before God for what we do with Christ, whether we accept Him as our Savior or reject Him."

Eddie Skeena listened, wide-eyed, as Ron turned to the Bible and began to read. He clung to every word with something that was close to desperation, but when Ron finished, he asked no questions. It didn't seem wise to say anything directly to him.

Up in the wheelhouse later that evening, Tip Russell talked with Ron about Eddie.

"I felt so sorry for him," the missionary's son said. "He didn't know what to do when we prayed. You know, I don't think he had ever heard anyone pray before."

"I thought the same thing myself when I saw him acting so bewildered. It's hard to believe that there are people like Eddie right here in Canada who have never heard the gospel of the Lord Jesus Christ."

The muscles in Tip's mouth tightened, but it was a while before he could speak.

"Know what, Ron?" he said. "Eddie Skeena is going right at the top of my prayer list."

CHAPTER 3

EXTRA DUTY

Ron Orlis took over at the helm until almost midnight when they reached an island where Charlie said it was all right to anchor for the night. Ron went below and crawled into his bunk. There was no noise aboard the *Good News* except for the rhythmic splash of waves against the hull. The next thing he knew it was morning and they were ready to get under way as soon as the tide was right.

After breakfast Eddie Skeena came up to the youthful American skipper. "What you want me to do now?"

The Orlis boy thought for a moment. There wasn't much work on board while they were on the water.

"I think I'm going to put you in the galley. How does that sound to you?"

"To cook?" The boy's eyes grew round. "Everybody get sick if Eddie Skeena cook." He held his stomach and grimaced expressively. "O-o-oh."

"We'll not have you cooking," Ron laughed. "You'll be peeling potatoes, washing dishes, doing anything the fellow who's cooking that day wants you to do."

The Indian boy scowled.

"Don't you have anything else, like steering boat?"

"I'm afraid not."

"That won't be so bad," Tip Russell put in. "I'll help you,"

"And," Ron added, "when we get to Old Factory, we'll expect you to help us load the boat or do whatever we have to do."

Toward noon Ron Orlis came on deck to see Charlie Eneveloe staring in the direction of the nearest land.

"When will we be into Old Factory, Charlie?" he asked, more to make conversation than anything else.

The pilot glanced at him disdainfully. "You are skipper. You have map and pencil. You tell Charlie."

The Orlis boy was silent momentarily.

"I've had some experience with boats, Charlie, but I'm new at a lot of it. I think you've seen that already. And I need your help."

The Indian's expression was immobile.

"We be into Old Factory after 2–3 hours, maybe. If wind not get too high."

"Do you expect the wind to blow today?"

He nodded.

"We have wind – plenty wind."

"How can you tell that?"

"See clouds over there?" He gestured in the direction

he had been looking where clusters of tiny cumulus clouds floated aimlessly about. "Those clouds say, 'plenty big on-shore wind some time this afternoon.'"

Ron nodded.

"Thanks, Charlie."

He remembered reading of those clouds, how they were formed by warm air rising off the land mass, and how the cool air from over the water would rush in to take the warm air's place. That spelled an on-shore wind. Charlie Eneveloe didn't know any of that, but he had learned to read those little white puffs of clouds. Ron's respect for the Indian pilot's knowledge grew.

Sure enough, before another hour passed the wind began to freshen. It came up slowly at first, scuffing the surface of the Bay into choppy little waves that deepened to swells as time wore on. The *Good News* began to buck and pitch over the broad-backed seas.

"You were right about the wind, Charlie," Ron said approvingly.

The Indian grunted.

"It is good we make shore. Plenty big blow tonight."

Finally, they pulled into the mouth of the river at Old Factory and up to the dock that had been put up in 1942 and was still standing.

"We're fortunate that this dock is sheltered from the wind," Ron observed as they tied up.

"It was planned that way," Charlie Eneveloe muttered tersely.

A handful of Indians, all that were left in the old settlement, came down, curiously, to see them.

Jay Russell turned to the young skipper.

"We'll soon see how much work has been done on tearing down the buildings," he said.

"Did you have a missionary come over and supervise the work?"

"That's what we wanted to do, but we didn't have anyone to spare. So, all we could do was find the most reliable man we could and put him in charge of a crew. I'm just hoping he went ahead with the work so we can start loading the first thing in the morning."

While they were standing there talking, Frank Thomas came up to them.

"I'm going out and get acquainted," he said.

Tip Russell and Eddie Skeena had already left the boat and were talking excitedly to the few Indian boys who were there.

Jay left the dock.

"Are you coming with me, Ron?" he asked.

"Sure thing."

They walked briskly over to the storm-bleached Hudson Bay buildings that were to be torn down.

"Doesn't look to me as though a thing's been done," Ron Orlis said.

"That's just what I was afraid of." Discouragement tinged the missionary's voice.

The Orlis boy walked about the sturdy building, looking it over carefully.

"These are certainly good, sound buildings. You'll get enough lumber to build several houses, won't you?"

"They'll save us a great deal of money," Jay Russell said. "In fact, getting them is making the difference between building homes so we can house new missionaries at these new stations we want to open up, and not being able to."

"I can see now why Danny and the Board were so anxious to have me come up and help."

"There's something else about these buildings that you don't see just by looking at them. There is nothing any better constructed in the whole North than Hudson Bay buildings. There is Econoboard three inches thick between the subfloor and the regular floor for insulation against the cold. And the walls and ceiling are well insulated. We haven't been able to afford to build our other houses the way we'll build these new ones." He sighed deeply. "If we can ever get the buildings torn down and the material transported to the new mission stations."

They turned back to the little Indian village and Jay sought out Marcel Tanana who had been responsible for getting the dismantling under way. Although the missionary's disappointment was keen, he did not show it.

"Nobody could come and work," Tanana said blandly. "White whale come. Everybody go hunt."

"You will get men to come tomorrow?"

"Oh, yes. We be there tomorrow." He spoke confidently,

as though he had not disappointed them by failing to do a thing in the three weeks since he had been hired.

The following day he did show up on the site with half a dozen Indians of varying ages and abilities. With them to help, Ron and Jay Russell and the two boys set to work dismantling the Hudson Bay Company store. Frank Thomas, who had come along to do personal work and hold evangelistic meetings was out on visitation and Charlie Eneveloe planted himself on deck and refused to move.

"Charlie's job to tell where rocks and reefs are," he announced with finality. "Not to make with the nails and hammer."

The work was slow and tedious, and the men worked long hours. When they finally dragged themselves, wearily, back to the boat, Frank Thomas had not yet come back. Supper was almost ready when he came in.

Ron went to meet him.

"Hi, Frank. How'd it go?"

"All right."

"Have you got a meeting set up for tonight?"

The Indian evangelist shook his head.

"No, there won't be any meeting tonight. And, to tell you the truth, I'm afraid there won't be a meeting here tomorrow night, either. These people are indifferent to the gospel. That's all. They don't know Christ as their Savior, and what's more, they act as though they don't care to know Him."

He took off his coat and they went into the gallery together.

"How did your work go?"

"You don't seem to be discouraged, Frank," Ron said curiously, ignoring the evangelist's question. "Doesn't it bother you to get a reception like that?"

"It used to." He pulled up a chair and sat down. "Then the Lord reminded me of how I used to be before I was saved. I couldn't care less about the things of God. But He kept working in my heart, and here I am."

"Work up here is discouraging, Ron," Jay put in. "We have some missionaries who have worked for years without winning a soul for Christ. The missionary couple who led Frank and his wife to the Lord worked for ten long years and they were the only fruit. But Frank has been instrumental in dealing with hundreds of his own people."

Eddie Skeena turned to Tip.

"You all the time say, 'win to Lord.' What that mean?"

"It means helping someone to see that he is a sinner," Tip explained, "and getting him to see that he is going to hell unless he confesses his sin and puts his trust in the Lord Jesus Christ to save him. It means getting him to become a Christian."

Charlie Eneveloe's face darkened angrily.

"It be better if you all go home." He stumbled noisily to his feet. "Go back home and leave Indian alone!"

He left the galley without eating and did not come back.

It was surprising how much work the crew was able to get done under supervision. The Indians worked carefully and willingly, and it wasn't long until they had torn down enough timbers and sheeting to fill the little schooner twice over. The lumber was carried aboard until the *Good News* was piled high with it.

"We will only be going to Paint Hills, Marcell," Jay said, "so we'll be back soon. We'll expect to pick up another load then and keep hauling until it is all hauled away."

"It be ready."

The wind had blown itself out during the several days it had taken Ron and the others to tear down the lumber for the first two trips. When they left the mouth of the river at high tide, the Bay lay before them like a small pond, reflecting the trees along the shore in its mirrored surface. With weather like that, the run up to Paint Hills was uneventful.

As they neared the site of the new mission station, Ron Orlis stood on the bow, shading his eyes against the glare of the brilliant summer sun.

"How are we going to unload this stuff, Jay?" he asked. "There isn't any dock."

The missionary chuckled good-naturedly.

"Just keep your eyes open, Ron," he said. "You're about to learn something you didn't know before."

Even as he spoke, two or three men were launching an odd craft into the water. It was made by lashing two large canoes to two poles that held them about 12 or 14 feet apart.

"We'll move in as close as we can," Jay said, "and they'll come out and haul the lumber in."

By the time the *Good News* had moved in and anchored, the canoes had reached her. They piled the canoes with lumber and, using an old outboard motor, pushed the load ashore. Ron and Jay Russell and the two boys went along to help with the unloading.

"I not know being a 'hand' is so hard work," Eddie Skeena said, surveying the blisters in his palms.

This was the first time they had unloaded the *Good News*, and it took them a little longer than they had planned on. Charlie Eneveloe came out on deck three or four times, surveying the water anxiously.

"We have to hurry," he announced. "Tide run out soon."

Ron Orlis looked at the dwindling pile of lumber still left on the boat.

"Another load and we'll be through."

The pilot shook his head.

"No time."

Ron Orlis saw that the tide had begun to run out. And they were only in a fathom of water.

"Stop the unloading!" he called out. "And, Frank, get the engine started."

He sprang forward to lift the anchor himself.

"Too late," Charlie said tersely.

Paying no attention to him, Ron heaved desperately on the anchor. The men flew to their stations. The canoes backed off and the *Good News* got under way. But that was all. As she came about there was a rasping shudder and she lurched to a halt.

Ron Orlis's stomach churned within him, and an icy knot came to his throat.

"Grounded," the Indian pilot announced. "Just like I told you."

CHAPTER 4

A CRY FOR HELP

Ron Orlis stared down at the tide as it rapidly ran out to sea. The *Good News* settled heavily into the sand.

"Do you think we've done any damage to the boat?" he asked numbly.

Charlie Eneveloe shrugged his shoulders.

"Who knows?"

Ron turned to Jay Russell who had just come up.

"If this isn't a stupid trick."

"I wouldn't worry about it if I were you. We're on sand, so there's no harm done. When some small schooners are damaged their owners will beach them on the sand this way in order to make emergency repairs. It just means that we've got to wait for high tide, that's all."

The pilot walked away, and Ron stared after him.

"I wonder why Charlie didn't tell me that?" he said pensively. "He acted as though he wanted me to get all shaken up."

"Charlie is different on this trip than he's been the other times we've used him," the missionary said. "I don't know whether he's under conviction, or whether there's something else that's bothering him."

In a short time, the water was gone around the *Good News*, except for a few scattered puddles. Gulls flocked in from everywhere, feeding noisily on the food left by the receding water.

Eddie Skeena poked his head up impishly from below. "Ron, you got wheels for boat so you run him on sand?" Ron Orlis flushed, but he laughed good-naturedly.

"Get along with you, Eddie, or I'll throw you overboard."

"Well," the missionary said presently, "I think we'd just as well anchor the boat and go ashore, don't you? We're going to have quite a wait until high tide."

They dropped anchor, checked its angle in the sand to be sure it would hold, and walked ashore. Eddie and Tip Russell hurried on ahead of them.

The Indian children, who had been watching the strange proceedings from shore, hung back shyly.

"They want to come up and talk to us," Jay said, "but they don't quite dare. Indian children are very shy."

"Shyness doesn't seem to bother them as far as Tip is concerned," Ron observed quietly. "Just look at the way they respond to him."

"He does get along with them in a wonderful way," the boy's father answered. "One reason, I think, is because he speaks Cree so well. He's as fluent in the language as an Indian."

"He would make a wonderful missionary up here, wouldn't he?"

"Yes, and I wouldn't be at all surprised if the Lord was already talking to him about it. He has a real compassion for them and is as burdened for their souls as we are."

Eddie Skeena said something that caused the kids to laugh and they all scampered up on the beach to a level area where they could play a game.

"I want to watch this," Ron Orlis murmured.

But before the game could get under way a gaunt, haggard Indian man came up to them. He had left his canoe on the sand out near the *Good News*.

"You not government supply boat?" Disappointment was thick in his voice.

"No," Jay Russell answered, "we're the *Good News*, the mission boat. You've heard of us, haven't you?"

The man ignored his question.

"You come from Moose Factory – from Moosinee?"

"We came up from Moose Factory a week or so ago. Why?"

"No government boat?" he persisted. "You no see boat?"

"We asked about her," Jay Russell answered, "but she hasn't come in there yet – or hadn't at the time we left. They didn't know what was wrong."

The man's expression did not change but hurt flickered in his eyes.

"Is there something wrong?"

For a time, he did not speak, and Jay had to repeat his question.

"No food," the Indian said simply. "There is no flour in barrel. We have no bread. Wife hungry. Children much hungry."

"How does it come that you do not have bread?" the missionary persisted, his voice firm. "Didn't you trap last winter? Didn't you catch skins?"

The Indian did not resent the questioning.

"I trap. Catch many skins. Good trap season."

"Then why don't you have bread?"

"Nobody have bread," the man who had identified himself as Steven Anniskette said. "Supply boat not come. Flour gone. Lard gone. Everybody hungry."

"Haven't you gone hunting?"

The Indian nodded.

"We hunt. Much hunt. Seals, they thin. Shoot, but, plunk!" With an expressive gesture he illustrated how the seal sank to the bottom when he was shot.

"This time of year, if a seal is shot near the water, he'll make it in and sink to the bottom. In the fall they're fat enough to come up again if they've been killed."

"We go out to sea. Look–Look." He shaded his eyes and pretended to scan the horizon. "No white whale. And in net – no fish."

Jay Russell continued to question the Indian. Steven Anniskette, he learned, lived in a village of about 75 or 100 people some 40 miles or so north of

Paint Hills. The warehouse was filled with fur and the men all had substantial credits with the Hudson Bay Company. The difficulty was that the boat that brought supplies in once a year, hadn't come yet.

"The airplane was supposed to bring flour, but fog keep away."

Satisfied that he had the whole story the missionary turned to Ron Orlis.

"I think we'd better look into this," he said. "There may be some real suffering up there." He switched to Cree. "We will come up to your village as soon as we finish unloading. We don't have much food along, but we can share what we have."

"I go now." The Indian did not thank them verbally, but with his eyes.

When he was gone the missionary turned to Ron.

"This is just the sort of thing we pray for," he said, his face glowing. "An opportunity to show the people Christianity at work."

"Do you think we brought along enough food to do any good for so many?" the Orlis boy wanted to know.

"First of all, we want to get up there and see just what the situation is. It may be that there are only a few cases of real hunger. If that's the case, we can give them enough food from our stores to last until supplies get here. Or we might be able to go to one of the other villages and get enough food to last until the supply boat arrives. It all depends on the extent of the need."

That night at high tide the *Good News* floated again. As the tide came in, Ron and the crew went out to the boat by canoe and took her out to deeper water.

"Look for two fathoms deep," Charlie Eneveloe said, taking soundings. "Always when you anchor on east side, two fathoms. Then plenty of water."

Early the next morning the canoes came out, took off the rest of the lumber, and the *Good News* began to plow north through jolting seas to the Indian village. Although practically empty and capable of ten knots or better, the heavy waves made it necessary to cut the speed. It was midafternoon when they finally arrived at the village where Steven Anniskette and his family lived. The Indian had gone ahead and brought the news that they were coming.

"Look at that crowd," Ron Orlis said as he worked the schooner in to the big dock on the river. "It looks to me as though everyone in the village is out."

Jay Russell nodded cryptically.

"Word spread that we promised to bring them food." Tip Russell looked up at the Indian evangelist who was standing next to him.

"Oh boy, Frank," he said, "this is your chance. Why don't you preach to them right now – before we even get off the boat? They're waiting to find out whether we've got anything to eat for them, or not. They'd listen to you."

Frank laughed.

"To tell you the truth, Tip, if I thought it would

do any good, I'd do it. But it's hard to get a man to listen when he's thinking about his stomach."

"Is this one of the places where we'll have a station, Jay?" Ron asked.

"We came over here and looked into the situation," he replied. "In several ways it would be an ideal location for a station. There's a good harbor here, and an improvised air strip which would give us good transportation. And there doesn't seem to be an excessive amount of fog, which would make it easy to get in and out by both boat and air. Then, too, it seems to be a central location. The trapping is comparatively good around here and a missionary stationed here would have access to reaching numbers of others who are outside the touch of the gospel."

"There must be some good reason for not coming in here or you surely would."

"It's the attitude of the people," Jay Russell continued. "They haven't been responsive to the gospel at all. In fact, there's real antagonism among them. More than we've found in most places where we haven't been too well received."

"They certainly seem friendly now," Ron said. "But, as you say, it's probably just the fact that we'll be seeing that they get food."

While they were talking, Charlie Eneveloe tossed a line to willing hands ashore and the *Good News* was secured to the dock. The village chief and Steven Anniskette came up to see Jay Russell and Ron Orlis.

"We only have a few supplies aboard," the missionary said, "but we will go back to Old Factory and get as much as we can spare of our own stores. Then we'll go to Rupert's House and Paint Hills and get enough from them to last you until the supply boat comes in."

The chief shook hands gravely.

"You are friend," he said.

When Frank Thomas came back from visitation late in the afternoon a broad smile lit his dark face.

"Well, how did it go?" Ron Orlis asked.

"I was better received here than any place we've stopped yet on this trip," he answered. "When you promised that we would help them, they saw that we were their friends. They won't forget."

He pulled up a chair and sat down.

"Were you able to talk to any of them about their souls, Frank?" Tip Russell put in.

"No, Tip. They weren't ready for that. I just tried to make friends first, and to ask them to come to the meeting tonight." A new light gleamed in his eyes. "We have the use of the old storehouse for a meeting tonight. Did you know that?"

Jay Russell shook his head incredulously.

"I can hardly believe it."

"I could hardly believe it, either, but I didn't have a bit of trouble."

Eddie Skeena eyed the evangelist queerly.

"Meeting?" he echoed. "What's that?"

"At a meeting we all get together and someone talks to us from God's Word," Frank began.

"Like devotions we have in galley every night?"

Frank thought for a moment.

"Well, something like that, only there's usually some singing and – why don't you come over tonight and you'll see just what a meeting is."

Charlie's face twisted contemptuously as Frank talked, but he said nothing.

They finished supper and did the dishes hurriedly. The announced time for the meeting was rapidly approaching. And though Frank had only been able to talk to half a dozen or so about the meeting. everyone seemed to know it and almost everyone was there. Some of the people had gone inside, but more were standing in clusters on the dock and along the river-bank, talking and waiting for the meeting to begin.

"It isn't every minister who can hold a service and have everyone in town there," Ron said.

"I just hope they have brought their hearts," the Indian evangelist said quietly, "instead of their curiosity."

"It looks as though everyone's here. We'd just as well start, hadn't we?"

"I'd think so." Frank turned on his heel. "If you want to get the people started inside, I'll go tell Jay and the boys that we're starting early."

Ron left the boat and walked diagonally away from the river's edge. He had almost reached the door to the storage building where they were holding services that night when suddenly there was a loud splash and a dozen or more excited cries all at once.

"Help!" someone shouted in Cree. "Somebody help!"

Ron Orlis didn't understand Cree, but he understood that cry. Whirling, he sprinted for the river's edge.

Two boys were in the fast-moving water, the bigger fellow trying desperately to hold the other's head above the swirling surface!

"Help!" the cry went up from the dock. "Help! Help!"

CHAPTER 5

MOCCASIN TELEGRAPH

For a brief, agonizing instant Ron Orlis froze motionless on the bank of the swift, cold river. They were only a mile or a mile and a half from the Bay and the tide was running out, making the current swift and terrible.

The graphic scene was unraveling before him, but it didn't seem real. It was too bewildering – too confusing.

Indians were running madly about, calling to one another, shouting for someone to come and help. No one seemed able to think clearly. One man tried to reach them by throwing out a line that was at least 20 feet too short. Two others shoved a canoe without paddles into the water and tried to pole it toward the hapless boy and his rescuer until, a dozen paces from shore, the water was too deep for their poles and they were swept helplessly along with the current in the opposite direction they would have had to go.

All of this happened quickly – in a moment of time.

In the water the fierce drama was being played in absolute silence. A young man of 19 or 20 battled frantically to cling to a lad about half his age and drag him to the bank. But fear had panicked the boy and he was struggling to free himself.

Ron Orlis kicked off his shoes, peeled off of his heavy jacket, and dove. Freezing cold enveloped his body and the current pulled and slammed at him with icy fingers. Surfacing, he fought against the current in a desperate attempt to reach the boys. He was thankful for the endless hours he had spent in the water at Angle Inlet as a kid, and the powerful stroke and kick Danny had taught him.

Doggedly, Ron swam against the current. The cold all but paralyzed his body and the exertion set his lungs aflame, but he could not slacken his pace. He had to keep driving forward, stroke by stroke by stroke.

Ron had almost reached them when the older boy could no longer maintain his grip on his wiry charge. Exhausted by the effort and extreme cold, he let his grasp relax momentarily. The boy chose that instant to give a quick twist and slipped away, going under the murky water. A brief cry of anguish escaped the lips of the would-be rescuer.

Ron saw the boy jerk free and go under, swept along by the powerful current.

He dove. The icy water was so murky he could see nothing, but he swung his arms about. His lungs screaming for air, he was about to come up when his wrist hit something! Grasping frantically, he got hold of a piece of cloth. It was the boy!

Ron pulled the Indian lad to him, got him by the arm, and surfaced.

By this time Tip Russell and Eddie Skeena had gotten the *Good News* lifeboat into the water and rowed rapidly over to Ron and his charge. Gratefully he grasped the little boat by the stern.

"Here, Ron," Tip cried. "We'll help you in."

"Don't do that. Just get us to the bank." Ron's teeth were chattering with cold, but he did not dare risk getting himself and the boy out of the water now.

A dozen hands reached eagerly down to help the boy and Ron Orlis out of the frigid water.

"Is he going to be all right?" someone asked.

"He opened his eyes."

The boy was breathing thinly and coughing. He would probably be sick. But, as the Indian said, he was going to be all right.

With a prayer of thanksgiving in his heart, Ron Orlis went aboard the *Good News* and changed into dry clothes. His lips were blue and goose flesh pimpled his arms and legs. He was still shivering violently.

"Are you all right, Ron?" Jay Russell demanded anxiously.

"If I ever get w-w-warm, I will be," he said.

"That was great!" Tip exclaimed, "I thought he was a goner when he got away from that Indian fellow, but you dove for him and came up with him. You saved his life."

About that time there was a footstep on the deck above and Frank Thomas came down and knocked lightly on the door of the cabin where Ron had just changed clothes.

"There's a fellow here who wants to talk to you, Ron," he said.

The Orlis boy opened the door to see a slight, dark-faced young Indian standing there.

"I bring you this." He handed Ron his New Testament. Water was still dripping from it.

Ron stared at it oddly.

"Where did you get this?" he asked.

"I find it in the water and think it your wallet," he explained. "I hold it in teeth to bring ashore. I not know it is little book."

"This book means more to me than quite a little money," Ron said, opening the soggy pages. "I can never thank you enough for bringing it to me. My sister gave it to me a little while before she died."

Then recognition gleamed in Ron's eyes.

"I thought I recognized you. You're the fellow who jumped in after the boy and held him up."

The Indian nodded.

"But if it not be for you, he drown." He thrust out his hand impulsively. "I am Johnny Goheen. I come to give thanks that you save my little brother."

Ron Orlis patted him on the shoulder.

They sat down in the little cabin and talked for a time, until Frank Thomas stuck his head in.

"We're an hour late, Ron, but I think we'll have the service anyway. Are you coming over?"

He turned to his guest.

"Wouldn't you like to come to the service, Johnny?"

They went over to the old storage building together. Although the service was late, almost everyone was still there and went into the building when Jay Russell announced the first song. The boy who had almost drowned, and his mother were missing, and so were the two men who floated almost out to sea in the canoe before someone thought to go after them. Everyone else was present.

The service was in Cree so Ron did not understand any of it, although Frank told him later that he preached on the uncertainty of man's time on earth and how no one knows how rapidly death can come.

Although Ron could not understand the language, it was easy to see that the people were moved. Eddie Skeena sat on the edge of his wooden bench; his chin tucked in his hands as he clung to every word. It was the same with Johnny Goheen. The lithe young man listened as though Frank were speaking only to him.

However, at the close of the meeting there were no hands for prayer. Ron was a bit disappointed, but it did not seem to bother the Indian evangelist.

"That is probably the first time in their lives that these people have ever heard the gospel," he said.

"They will have to have time to think it over, to understand just exactly what it means."

The following morning when they put out to sea the villagers were all down to wave goodbye to them. Eddie Skeena, who had helped with the lines, came into the wheelhouse and stood beside Ron Orlis.

"Ron," he began seriously, "if Robert Goheen had drowned last night, would he have gone to heaven like Frank talk about, or would he go to other place?"

Ron was silent for a moment.

"The Bible tells us that only those who have taken the Lord Jesus Christ as their Savior will go to heaven," Ron told him. "I don't know Robert Goheen, so I don't know whether he is a Christian or not. But from what I've heard about the village, I'd have to say that I doubt whether he has ever accepted Christ."

The boy thought about that a moment or two, seriously.

"If something happen to me," he ventured timidly, "would I go to heaven?"

"That would depend on whether you had accepted Christ as your Savior or not, Eddie," the Orlis boy continued. "You see, it doesn't make any difference how good you are or how bad you are, God has the same means of salvation for everyone...."

Ron wanted to press the subject further, but Tip Russell came by just then and called to Eddie. The two boys went off together.

They decided to run all the way down to Old

Factory that night so they could start loading supplies the next morning and get to Rupert's House and Paint Hills and back up to Thompson with a load of food as soon as possible. For that reason, they took turns at the wheel. At ten o'clock, although it was still light, Eddie Skeena and Tip Russell turned in. Jay was at the helm and Ron Orlis, Frank, and Charlie Eneveloe were in the galley drinking coffee.

"I had a little talk with Eddie this morning, Frank," Ron Orlis said. "Your message last night really got him to doing a lot of thinking."

Charlie scowled into his coffee and grunted his disapproval, but he said nothing.

"That's good," Frank replied. "I'll try to have a talk with him as soon as I can."

"I wish I could have understood that message of yours, Frank. The way Eddie and Johnny Goheen listened to it, it must have been something that really spoke to their hearts."

"I felt that God was using it," Frank said. "I am anxious to get back up to Thompson. When we go in there with food, I'm praying that there will be another good opportunity to talk with them about Christ. They'll have had a little time to think over what was said last night."

Charlie got to his feet to get himself another cup of coffee. As he did so, he almost spilled some on the Indian evangelist's arm. Ron, who was watching him, could not be sure whether he had done it purposely or not.

"You think it go so good for you next time you go to Thompson," Charlie blurted derisively. "You think you make Christians out of everybody. Not be too sure. It not go like you think. You see."

"What do you mean?" Ron asked irritably.

"Peter Hoonah, he medicine man at Thompson," Charlie said, his lips curling bitterly about the words. "He away when we there. He know what you do. He think you try for make Christians out of his people. He no like. He come back to make trouble. Plenty trouble."

Ron Orlis's forehead crinkled quizzically.

"If this Peter Hoonah was away when we were there," he said, "how does he know that we had a service? Did someone go and tell him?"

Charlie shook his head. "Moccasin telegraph."

Ron Orlis blinked but did not comment. He had heard people in the north mention moccasin telegraph in jest. Usually, they talked of gossip that seemed to be without beginning or end. But that wasn't what Charlie had reference to. It was an amazing means of communication that some Indians seemed to have. While there were those white men who scoffed at it, most of the northland missionaries Ron knew recognized that it existed even while they admitted they had no explanation or understanding of it.

"Did you see this Peter Hoonah before we left Thompson this morning?" Ron asked.

The Indian pilot shook his head.

"Then how do you know that he is coming to cause us trouble when we put into the river with supplies?"

The same answer came back. "Moccasin telegraph." With that he whirled and stormed out. A moment later he opened the galley door a crack.

"You going to have trouble," he said prophetically. "You going have plenty trouble."

CHAPTER 6

TROUBLE WITH HOONAH

Ron Orlis excused himself as soon as possible and went out to the wheelhouse where Jay Russell was on duty. The veteran missionary had his Bible open and was reading snatches as he could.

"Hi, Ron, beautiful night, isn't it?"

The Orlis boy came inside and closed the door behind him. "Seen Charlie Eneveloe around anywhere?" he asked.

"He came up 10 minutes or so ago," Jay Russell replied "and is sitting back in the fantail. I thought he was probably coming to take over the wheel, but he didn't."

Ron leaned against the bulkhead, and for the space of two or three minutes, said nothing.

"Think we're going to be able to make it to Old Factory before dark?" Jay asked.

"I think so. According to the way I've got it figured we should be getting fairly close now."

Once more he lapsed into silence.

Jay noted it.

"You're awfully quiet, Ron," he said. "Is there anything wrong?"

"We just had another little run-in with Charlie."

"I'm beginning to wish we had gotten one of the other pilots," the missionary said. "There's no doubt, but that Charlie's the best in this section of James Bay, but he's getting more difficult to be around all the time." He checked the compass once more and corrected their heading slightly.

"Charlie seems to think that we're going to have some trouble when we go back to Thompson," Ron continued. "He says an old Indian medicine man by the name of Peter Hoonah is going to give us a real bad time."

"Old Peter Hoonah is from Thompson," Jay said. "I'd forgotten all about him."

"Do you know him?"

"Know him?" the missionary echoed, his voice rising. "Every missionary on the east coast of the Bay gets to know Peter Hoonah sooner or later. He's the most evil, ruthless old man you will find anywhere in the whole territory. He hates Christians and especially missionaries, with the passion of Satan."

"That fits."

"Peter Hoonah is one man who is in a good position to cause us trouble," Jay Russell went on. "The Indians are all afraid of him and his so-called 'power' as a medicine man."

"Charlie says that Hoonah found out through moccasin telegraph that we were in the village talking to the people about the Savior." Ron Orlis paused, waiting expectantly.

No answer.

"Charlie also said he found out by the same method, moccasin telegraph, that Hoonah was going to cause us trouble on our next trip."

For the space of a minute or two Jay Russell said nothing.

"I suppose you'd like to know what I think about moccasin telegraph," he continued after a time.

"I sure would. I've heard about it, but I'd never given it much thought until this evening."

"To tell you the truth, I don't like to talk much about it because I don't understand it," the missionary went on. "There could be some very simple explanation for it, a means of communication that we whites know nothing about. Or it might be something else. All I know is that there seems to be some form of communication among certain Indians that is beyond us." He took a deep breath and expelled the air thoughtfully. "Of course, in this particular case Charlie Eneveloe wouldn't have needed any means of communication to know what Peter Hoonah's reaction would be to the gospel being preached in his own village. Everyone knows how Hoonah has fought us at every turn."

"You think he actually will try to cause us trouble, then. Is that it?"

Jay nodded emphatically.

"I most surely think he will do everything he can to interfere with the meeting and stop the people from attending. If he is back in the village when we get there, he could cause us plenty of trouble."

Ron Orlis straightened and stepped forward to peer out into the spreading darkness. "I think I see the river."

Jay nodded. "I saw it a few minutes ago," he said. He brought the *Good News* about 30 degrees to angle for the Old Factory River where they would tie up for the night. "Ron, please don't say anything to Eddie or Tip about any of this. There's no use to frighten them."

"I won't say a word."

A couple of minutes later Charlie came in and took the helm to bring the schooner safely past the reefs and into the mouth of the Old Factory River. He looked at Ron coldly but did not speak to him.

Although Jay Russell had asked Ron not to say anything to Tip and Eddie about Peter Hoonah, no one had had breakfast the next morning before the boys got him off to one side and questioned him excitedly.

"What's this about that old medicine man, Peter Hoonah, trying to stop Frank from preaching when we get back to Thompson?" Tip Russell wanted to know.

Ron Orlis's eyes narrowed.

"Who said anything about Peter Hoonah?"

"Come on, Ron, we know about him, so there's no use in keeping it a secret." The boy's eyes were dancing with excitement. "Is he really going to try to stop Frank from preaching up there?"

"You think there be big fight, maybe?" Eddie Skeena put in hopefully.

"Now listen, you guys," the Orlis boy said sternly, "I want to know how you found out about Peter Hoonah and what he is going to try to do."

Eddie's homely face twisted into a grin.

"Moccasin telegraph," he said.

Ron Orlis blinked his eyes incredulously.

"Moccasin telegraph?"

"That's right," Tip continued, "Moccasin telegraph. Only it didn't have to travel too far. You see, we were sleeping right under the wheelhouse when you and Dad were talking last night. So come on, out with it. Tell us the whole story."

"You rascals!" Ron Orlis exploded good-naturedly. "I should pitch you both overboard."

They loaded most of their own supplies onto the *Good News* and went up to Rupert's House where they explained the situation to the local chief and the white manager of the Hudson Bay Store.

"Of course, we'll help," the manager said. "We had no idea that anyone near us was short of food."

They loaded on the flour and lard and other foodstuffs Rupert's House could spare and went on up to Paint Hills. There was no Hudson Bay store at that little outpost, but the chief and council gave Thompson a portion of their supplies.

"You tell them if that not enough, come back," the chief said.

Although Jay Russell made arrangements to get supplies from Paint Hills that night, it was morning at high tide before they could bring the stores out to the schooner.

"You not go closer?" Eddie Skeena asked, a gentle taunting note in his voice. "Tip and I want to play in sand."

"Well, I don't care to play in the sand again," the young skipper told him. "And that's for sure."

Charlie Eneveloe said little to Ron Orlis during their trip up the coast, but the closer they got to Thompson the more his uneasiness grew.

"Why you not tell Frank he not try to preach tonight?" the Indian pilot blurted suddenly.

"I can't do that. The meeting is all arranged. The chief and council gave their permission."

"Tell Frank there just be trouble. Tell him Hoonah make plenty bad medicine. Tell him wait for next trip. Hoonah, him gone, maybe."

"I know how you feel about it, Charlie," Ron Orlis said, "but we have to hold the service. That's the reason we're up here. We're trying to help your people, to win them to Christ so they can be saved and go to heaven."

Hurt and fear leaped to the pilot's eyes and mingled there. "Why you not leave Indian alone?" he demanded suddenly. "Why you preach to him all time?"

"Because the Bible tells us that everyone is lost and

headed for an eternity in hell unless they confess their sin and put their trust in the Lord Jesus Christ as their Savior," he explained carefully. "That applies to the Indian as well as to the white man. That is the reason the missionaries are here – because they love you."

Charlie Eneveloe started. A strange look that Ron could not read came into his eyes. When he spoke, there was fire in his voice, but it was not the burning, hating fire of old. His heart was not in it.

"Jesus white man's God. We have Indian god."

"Jesus is the white man's God," the young American said. "He is also the God of the Indian. The Bible says, 'for there is no other name under heaven that has been given among men by which we must be saved.'"

Charlie's gaze met Ron's, bewilderment and uncertainty rearing in his eyes. Then he strode forward roughly and took the helm.

"All right!" he exploded. "Try to have service! Get much trouble from Peter Hoonah. It not Charlie Eneveloe's fault if it happen."

Ron turned and stared out the window at the gathering Indians. Was old Peter Hoonah out there?

As though reading his thoughts, Tip Russell came in and stood beside him.

"Do you see the old medicine man out there, Ron?" he whispered.

The youthful American shook his head.

"What do you think he's going to do?" the boy persisted.

It began to look as though the old medicine man was not going to do anything at all. Steven Anniskette and Johnny Goheen were the first aboard when the *Good News* tied up. They had gathered a crew together and were not long in getting the supplies ashore.

"Again, it is our thanks to you," Johnny said when the task was completed. "Now no one go hungry. Stomachs get full."

"We're glad for that," Ron answered.

"Here is Robert. He well now."

Only then did Ron notice the slight Indian lad who was standing beside Johnny.

"That's fine." Ron put his hand on the boy's shoulder and Robert smiled up at him. "Did you get rid of all that water you swallowed?"

Johnny Goheen broke in.

"Him not talk English." For a couple of minutes Johnny translated for both of them.

Ron Orlis was so busy talking to the likable little Indian lad that he did not see or hear anyone approach until an aged voice rasped out.

"What you doing here?"

Robert Goheen fell back, his small face ashen and his eyes wide with terror. Ron's head jerked around to stare up into two piercing black eyes sunk far back in an ugly, bony face. No need to ask who this was. Ron got to his feet.

"My name's Ron Orlis," he said, thrusting out his hand.

Peter Hoonah's gaze did not waver. Neither did he touch Ron's hand with his own gnarled fingers.

"What you doing here?" he lashed out again.

"We came to bring supplies to the people," Ron said evenly, ignoring the uneasiness that welled in an icy knot to his throat. "The supply boat hasn't come up yet and the flour and lard have about given out. So, we took some of our own stores, some from Rupert's House and some from Paint Hills. The chief says he thinks you will have enough to last now until the supply boat arrives."

The wicked face pressed closer to his, eyes flashing their hatred.

"You lie!" He spat out the words.

"I guess it doesn't matter whether you believe me or not," Ron said evenly. "But it happens to be the truth. And I think everyone else here knows it."

"You not come for bring supplies," the old medicine man snarled, "you come for preach. You come for take people away from Indian ways!"

"We came to bring supplies," the Orlis boy corrected him, "but we do plan on having a service tonight. I don't deny that. And we're going to preach Christ to the people. I won't deny that, either."

"You not have service!" the old man's voice raised to a shout. "You not preach! Understand?"

CHAPTER 7

HOONAH'S SHAKING TEPEE

Ron Orlis looked down at the angry medicine man. "You not have preaching!" he rasped. "I, Peter Hoonah, forbid it!"

Ron did not answer him.

By this time, a crowd of curious, half-frightened Indians had gathered around. The medicine man pressed closer to the young American, evil wreathing his ugly features. Rage flamed his eyes and set his lips to trembling. For an instant he seemed transfixed. Suddenly he stabbed a bony finger into Ron's face.

"You have preaching and evil spirits get angry," he hissed in warning. "Peter Hoonah make bad medicine!"

Fear settled over the people like a cloud. Ron could feel their apprehension.

"We intend to have the service tonight, Peter," he said quietly. "We are not afraid of the evil spirits or your bad medicine."

Peter Hoonah purpled with rage. So angry was he that for a moment he could not speak.

"You see!" he cried, his voice breaking. "You see what happen! You have service and Peter Hoonah make bad medicine against you. He make bad medicine against anyone who goes!" He turned to the crowd and raised his voice to a shout. "You hear that? Peter Hoonah make bad medicine against anyone who go to hear preaching!"

With that he switched into Cree.

Charlie Eneveloe, who had been standing on the fringe of the crowd, listening, was sallow and shaken, and his dark face ringed with sweat despite the stiff, cool breeze.

Jay Russell came out on deck.

"What was that all about, Ron?" he wanted to know.

The Orlis boy forced a weak grin to his lips.

"I just met Peter Hoonah. And believe me, he's all you said he is, and more."

They all went below, and he told Jay Russell and Frank Thomas all that had happened.

"I'm not surprised," Frank said. "I'm not surprised at all. The medicine man knows that once a fellow accepts Christ as his Savior he no longer has any hold over him. There's nothing that will put a medicine man out of work quicker than the Lord Jesus Christ working in the hearts of the people."

"Believe me, old Peter Hoonah is not going to be put out of business without a fight," Ron Orlis answered, "and that's for sure."

"Of course, this is just the opening round," Jay Russell observed. "It's the warning. Hoonah's going to try us and see if we scare first. That's always part of their plans. They win over half their battles through stark fear."

"We cannot back down," Frank Thomas said quickly. "We've got to have that service tonight, even though nobody shows up for it. If we don't, Peter will have the upper hand. He'll boast to the people that the evil spirits overcame the Christ of the white men, and they could not hold their service. The whole future of what we do or are able to do for the Lord here at Thompson rests on what we do tonight."

At that moment Charlie Eneveloe lurched into the boat and came down to where they were sitting.

"Charlie!" Jay cried, leaping to his feet. "What's the matter?"

The man's lower jaw sagged, and it was the space of a minute before he could speak. Ron thought at first that he had been drinking, but he soon realized that was not the case.

"What's the matter?" Jay repeated.

"Peter Hoonah, he talk to me!" he blurted, suddenly finding voice. "He say he do 'shaking tepee' tonight if you not stop service!"

"What?" Ron cried.

"He do 'shaking tepee!' He bring evil spirits right into village!" Charlie, still trembling violently, grasped for a chair and sat down.

"What is this 'shaking tepee'?" Ron Orlis asked.

"You know," Jay answered, "I've lived up here more than ten years and I've never seen it."

Frank Thomas shook his head and for a brief instant it seemed that fear gleamed in his eyes.

"It is not a good thing," he said. "It is very bad. And the way Hoonah is using it, it will terrify everyone."

Tip Russell was waiting for Ron Orlis on deck. Eddie Skeena was standing nearby, staring down at the water.

"Say, Ron," the missionary's son began, "what did you do when you went ashore a little while ago? You sure must've kicked up a storm."

"What makes you say that?"

"Eddie and I went ashore ourselves right after you came back on board and the kids were afraid to talk to us. They'd just look at us and scoot the other way."

"I wouldn't worry about it if I were you, Tip. It'll all work out."

"Did old Peter Hoonah have anything to do with it?" Tip asked. "Did he?"

The Orlis boy nodded.

Eddie Skeena looked up. His eyes were usually warm and friendly but now they were cold, defiant.

"I told you it was Peter Hoonah!" he said, eyeing Ron accusingly. "Bad things will come to the village tonight."

Not long afterward, Jay Russell called his son and Eddie to one side and told them that he wanted them to stay aboard unless one of the men was with them.

"But Dad," Tip protested.

"I think that's best, Tip. Let's not argue about it."

The boys spent the balance of the afternoon, restlessly, on deck, but Jay Russell and Ron and Frank Thomas spent the time on their knees in prayer.

"Do you think Peter will come over and check to see if we're going to go ahead with the service tonight?" Ron asked as they all sat about the table in the galley.

Frank shook his head.

"He's had experience with missionaries before," he said. "He's not going to check because he already knows that it isn't likely that we have been frightened out of holding our service tonight."

"What time will he have this 'shaking tepee,' or whatever it's called?" Ron asked presently.

"I think we'll know," Frank said, "by watching the people. He'll get them all out for it." He glanced down at his watch. "My guess is that it will be an hour or so before our service is to start."

Sure enough, the crowd began to gather on the edge of the village about 7 o'clock. Ron saw it and hurried back to the galley.

"Better hurry," he called, "it looks as though they're getting ready to go."

As they stepped off the boat, Jay Russell turned to the Indian evangelist. "Do you think it's all right for us to go and watch?" he asked. "Will it have any bad effect on the people if they see us there?"

Frank shook his head.

"I think it is much better if we go than if we stay on board the boat. By going we'll show Hoonah and the people that we aren't afraid of the old medicine man. If we stay away there is no knowing what he will make them believe about us."

Tip Russell and Eddie Skeena hurried to catch up with Ron.

"Have you ever seen anything like this before?" Tip asked.

The Orlis boy shook his head.

"Neither Dad nor I have seen it, either, but Eddie has. Haven't you, Eddie?"

"You weren't supposed to tell."

"I–I'm sorry. Ron won't say anything about it to anyone, anyway. Will you, Ron?"

The village was deserted as Ron and the others walked through it to the place where the old Indian medicine man was preparing for his demonstration. Although he was working steadily, a smile lighted his crafty old face as he saw the missionaries and the two boys come up.

Peter Hoonah had already selected three small spruce trees that formed a crude triangle with each side about six feet long. He cut off the branches, leaving only the limber tree trunks. Then he pulled them together at the top and bound them there with a thong of moosehide. Once that was accomplished, he took huge chunks of bark he had gathered that afternoon and fastened them in place to form the covering for the crude tepee. As the work progressed, the apprehension among the watching Indians crescendoed. Talk died away and they began to cast nervous glances about, as though they wanted to leave, but dare not.

At last, the old medicine man finished his work. He stopped momentarily and straightened. A taut, electric silence ran over the group.

Then he moved deliberately through the crowd to the place where the missionaries were standing. The Indians fell back in silence on either side to give him a wide berth.

"Call off meeting now!" he intoned in a voice that sent a shudder through his listeners. "Save yourselves and these!"

"The meeting goes on," Frank Thomas told him.

"Then you will be responsible. We hold you accountable for all that happen!" He swayed slightly in the breeze. "You and you alone be responsible!" He raised his voice to a shout. "Stay and see the displeasure of the evil spirits in the tepee!"

"I think we made a mistake in coming down here," Jay whispered cautiously.

Frank shook his head. "This man is clever. If we hadn't come, he'd have used that. He is a very clever man."

Tip Russell tugged at Ron's heavy Indian sweater.

"This gives me the creeps already."

"Just wait," Eddie warned him.

Old Peter Hoonah turned slowly, his dark eyes swords that drove through those upon whom he fastened them. From one side to the other he looked until the excitement and suspense were as taut as circus tightwires. Only then did he stoop and duck quickly inside.

The Indians watching, scarcely dared to breathe.

"Now what happens?" Ron Orlis asked.

"The old medicine man is supposed to go into a trance," Jay Russell answered. "I've never seen anything like this before, but I've heard the Indians describe them."

As though on signal, they began to hear the weird, mournful chanting of the medicine man inside the improvised tepee.

Even the wind seemed to fear what was happening. It stopped its restless stirring in the tops of the trees and waited, hushed and expectantly for the demonstration to continue.

So taut, so emotion-charged was the scene that Ron Orlis felt his pulse quicken and his breath come in short, quick gasps.

A wolf howl pierced the taut silence and Tip Russell jumped.

"What was that? What was that?"

"Sh-sh-sh-sh." Ron put a hand on the boy's shoulder.

The wolf howl sounded again only louder. This time there was no mistaking it. It came from the tepee the medicine man had entered. A second wolf joined the first, barking and snapping like an animal on attack. A caribou bugled noisily, and a bear growled in warning.

Coming one at a time, at first the sounds intermingled one with another until it was all but impossible to separate them. They crescendoed in intensity and as they did so, the tepee began to shake. The shaking, too, started gently, a mere quivering of bark at first and a shimmer of spruce trunks.

Gulls and geese cried one to another from inside the tepee and sounded as though they were fighting noisily for food. The piercing note of the loon climbed above the melee as beaver, lynx, mink, and wolverine added to the din.

The shaking of the tepee began slowly enough but built up rapidly. It quivered and shook like a thing possessed. Bark rattled noisily against bark, and tremored with ever-increasing violence.

It was not until the babble of human voices in strange, discordant tongues were added, however, that the tepee began to lurch.

But lurch, it did.

It threw itself from side to side, jerking at the sapling roots that held it down, flinging itself like an anchored boat is hurled about in a hurricane, flinging itself until Ron Orlis was sure the roots would lose their hold in the soil and let the tepee collapse and fall about old Peter Hoonah.

Tip Russell reached up and grasped Ron's arm, squeezing it tightly. The Indians watching were as white as death.

The sounds cut off abruptly in mid-breath. The

tepee ceased its shaking. The hush of midnight exploded over the stunned crowd.

And then the weird mumble of Hoonah's chanting filled the air. It was not a loud chant. Only the hush it shattered made it seem so. At last, that, too, died away and all was silent once more.

Still the crowd did not move.

"What do you make of it, Ron?" Jay Russell asked softly.

"I wish I knew. Gives a fellow an eerie feeling, doesn't it?"

"Think one man could make all those noises?"

"Not if he had all of his own and his wife's relatives in the tepee with him."

"It's like I was telling you about moccasin telegraph," the missionary continued. "There might be a very simple human explanation to something like this and there might not."

"Look at these people around us," the Orlis boy whispered, "they don't buy the idea that there's a simple human explanation for it."

Old Peter Hoonah came out and stood there for a moment, blinking his eyes. Then he fastened his gaze upon Ron Orlis and his companions.

"You see the power of the spirits," he grated. "That power will be turn loose on you if you have preaching tonight!" his voice became hollow. "Leave Thompson and live!"

Jay Russell spoke up quickly in Cree so all could understand.

"We are going to leave Thompson at high tide tomorrow just as we planned," he said. "And tonight, we are having our service just as we planned. You are all invited."

A gasp went up from the crowd.

Peter Hoonah stood there, trembling with rage.

"Come on," Jay said quickly, touching Ron on the arm. "We've gained a little advantage. The people are astonished at the fact that we would dare stand up to Hoonah in the face of such a demonstration and have our services. Let's get in and start before that wily old rascal thinks of something else."

They walked quickly back to the storage building and went inside.

"I'll go get the portable organ, Frank," Ron Orlis said,

"I–I don't know if I–I want to stay tonight for meeting," Eddie Skeena said uncertainly.

Tip eyed him, a taunt in his voice.

"What's the matter, are you scared?"

"Th-th-there won't be anyone else here."

"Sure there will. I'll be here and so'll Dad and Ron Orlis."

"You know what I mean."

CHAPTER 8

TROUBLE WITH GOOD NEWS

Reluctantly, Eddie Skeena sat back down and waited. In a moment, Ron Orlis returned from the *Good News* with the portable organ and the service began. Only Ron and the two boys were in the audience when they sang the first song. They started the second and there was an uncertain shuffling at the door.

Ron heard it and ventured a quick glance. It was Johnny Goheen. Thank God that at least one of the villagers dared to come. They hopefully sang a third number and a fourth, but no one else dared to brave the old medicine man's wrath.

Once, just before Frank started to preach, old Peter Hoonah came to the door and looked in. Frank gave no indication that he even saw him. The Indian evangelist preached as though the building was crowded to the rafters. When the service was over, he gave no altar call, but went down to talk to Johnny.

"Thank you for coming," he said.

The boy's face was pale, but his voice was firm. "Old Hoonah don't scare me."

"It took a lot of courage for you to come here tonight – the only one."

"No more than for you to have service," the Indian lad said.

There was a brief hesitation.

"If you decide you would like to talk to someone about taking Christ as your Savior, I'll be glad to talk to you."

"I know." And then he was gone.

"Well," Jay Russell said when they were back on board the *Good News* that night, "today's over and I'm sure glad of that, I can tell you."

"How do you think it came off?" Ron Orlis asked.

"Not too bad." The missionary sat down and crossed his legs. "We showed Peter Hoonah and the people here in Thompson that we're not afraid of him or anything he can do. We went ahead and held our church service in defiance of him."

"With an audience of one," the Orlis boy reminded him. "Everybody else was too scared to come."

"We had one person from the village – Johnny Goheen. But don't forget that Eddie Skeena was there, too. He's an Indian and just a boy. When the people get to thinking about those things and realize that both Johnny and Eddie are getting along all right it's bound to have an effect on them."

"If nothing else happens," Frank put in.

"Do you expect something else to happen?" Ron asked quickly.

"Let's look at it this way," the evangelist said. "Peter Hoonah is one of the most crafty individuals in the whole northland. He's tried once and hasn't succeeded in getting his way. Do you think he's done everything he knows how to do?"

"I see your point."

Jay Russell nodded.

"I had been hoping that we'd seen the end of the old rascal," the missionary said, "but now that you explain it that way, Frank, I see that we're still in for trouble."

"We certainly are," Frank continued. "I know my people and I know the medicine men and the way they operate. There are no more crafty people in the world than Indian medicine men."

"Think we should post a guard on the boat tonight?" Ron asked.

"That's an excellent idea," the veteran missionary said. "Hoonah may try something on board." He got to his feet. "I'll take the first four hours."

There was a short period of silence.

"I wish we knew what to expect from him," Frank Thomas said uneasily. "Then we'd know what to guard against. But we don't. We don't have the slightest idea what he might try to do."

Although they posted a guard aboard the *Good News* all night long, all was peaceful. No one even came near the boat.

"Well," Ron Orlis said as he went down to the galley for breakfast, "we'd just as well have stayed in bed all night."

"I feel better having watched the boat," Jay answered. "I tell you, Ron, we aren't dealing with just an ordinary fellow who has a grudge against us. Peter Hoonah is as unscrupulous as he is dangerous."

Frank, who was serving as cook that day, set a plate of bacon on the table.

"We'll be out of here in a little while. Then we won't have to worry about him until we decide to come back again."

Tip stuck his head in the doorway just then.

"Hi, everybody."

"Where's your pal?" his dad asked. "We're about ready to eat and we want to hurry so we can get under way."

"Eddie's here." Tip looked around. "But where's Charlie? Did he go out somewhere?"

"Charlie?" Jay Russell echoed. "Isn't he in his bunk?"

"He wasn't there half a second ago."

Jay Russell's gaze met Ron's and held there.

"Did he go out while you were on guard?"

The Orlis boy shook his head.

"Nope. Nobody went out when I was up on deck."

"And I didn't see anyone, either," Jay said, "when I took my turn at guard."

They stared numbly at one another.

"He was frightened last night," Frank observed. "He was so frightened I couldn't even talk to him."

"Do you suppose he's run out?" Ron asked.

"That's the way it looks to me."

Ron Orlis put both hands heavily on the table.

"Wh-wh-what are we going to do?" he asked, his voice taut. "We can never run the *Good News* without a pilot to show us where the reefs and sandbars are. We'd have her aground in 24 hours."

Jay put on his jacket.

"I'm going out to see if I can find Charlie. I think we can talk him into coming back."

Ron stood.

"I'll go with you."

A brisk on-shore wind was whipping in from the Bay as they left the schooner and made their way past the storage building where they had the service the night before. They met an Indian on the path and spoke to him. His lips parted slightly, as though to speak. Then fear gleamed in his dark eyes, and he quickened his pace to push past them.

"Old Hoonah did his work well last night," Jay said quietly. "That fellow wanted to speak to us, but at the last minute he didn't dare."

"The old medicine man got next to Charlie Eneveloe, too," Ron said.

"There's no doubt in my mind about that. He was too clever to try to sabotage the boat, although I wouldn't have put it past him if he thought he could get away with it. But all he had to do was get hold of Charlie and scare him out of going with us."

"Why do you think he'd do that?" Ron asked. "If we don't have a pilot we'd have to stay here in Thompson and he wants to be rid of us. It looks to me as though that would defeat his purpose."

"I'd thought of that, too. Then I realized that Peter Hoonah wants to be rid of us completely. He's not just thinking of Thompson. He knows that as long as we are on the Bay, we're a threat to him, so he wants us out of here."

Jay Russell took a deep breath.

"This is the way I've got it doped out. He figures that he's got the people here so scared they won't have anything to do with us – at least for a while. He's deprived us of our pilot. We'll fool around here for a few days thinking that we'll find somebody to take over in that department. When we can't find anyone, I think he is counting on our deciding that we will try to run the boat ourselves. Then we'll take her out and pile her up somewhere."

"That sounds logical."

"So, we'd better pray that we're able to find Charlie and that he'll go with us."

"You can say that again."

An hour later they found Charlie Eneveloe in a little house on the edge of the village. He came to the door, terror still gleaming in his dark eyes.

"No!" he exploded passionately. "I not go! Evil spirits angry. Much angry! I not go on boat!"

"Now, Charlie," Jay said evenly, "Peter Hoonah

gave us warning of all sorts of terrible things that would happen to us if we held the service last night. We went ahead anyway and look at us. Nothing has happened. We're just as well now as we've ever been. If he was going to do anything – if he was able to do anything he'd have done it last night."

"Peter Hoonah not through yet," Charlie warned. "Evil spirits not through yet."

"He's just trying to scare you."

For an instant Charlie remained silent.

"You promised to pilot us," Jay reminded him. "You gave your word. Our agreement with you is that you'll guide for the summer. That is the way we are paying you. If you don't stay with us, we won't be under any obligation to pay you for what you have already done."

The Indian seemed to be wavering until an aged voice spoke sharply to him from somewhere within the house. Instantly the pilot's resolve stiffened.

"Of what good is money if your bones are bleaching on shore?"

Both Ron and Jay tried to persuade him to change his mind, but their efforts were useless.

"I guess that does it," Ron said as they turned, at last, to make their way back to the *Good News*. "We might have known it. Peter Hoonah isn't taking any chances. He got hold of Charlie and is staying with him to make sure he doesn't weaken and go with us."

"Now we've got a real problem on our hands," Jay said.

"Do you think we can find anyone who knows the Bay to guide us?"

"We'll have to try, of course." The missionary's face was ashen with concern. "But I don't know where we're going to find anyone to do it. Everyone except Johnny Goheen was afraid to go to the service last night. I'm sure we're not going to be able to get them to come aboard with us in the face of Peter Hoonah's threats."

For two or three minutes they walked on dejectedly.

"Think it would do any good to go and see Johnny Goheen?" Ron asked, finally.

"I don't know. What did you have in mind?"

"I thought maybe he would know of someone who would act as pilot for us. Someone who didn't live here in Thompson."

"It wouldn't hurt to try."

They found the young Indian at his home not far from the river. He was sitting on the front step cleaning his rifle when they came up and told him what they wanted.

His forehead crinkled thoughtfully, and he scratched at his ear with a forefinger.

"There's old Ray Mirasty," he said. "He know Bay good. Maybe not so good as Charlie, but he know."

"Do you think he'd go with us?"

Johnny shook his head.

"Maybe. But maybe no. He was scare last night. He was much scare!"

"Do you know of anyone in any of the other villages?" Jay asked.

"No. Nobody I know, except maybe one fella. Him down by Moose Factory."

"That's a long way away."

"Him there, maybe. Maybe not. I see when I on government boat last season."

Jay Russell's eyes lit.

"You were on the government boat last year?" he echoed, excitement raising his voice. "Do you know anything about the Bay, Johnny? Do you know where the reefs and harbors are?"

"Little bit, maybe."

"Do you think you could guide for us? We are only going to Paint Hills, Rupert's House, Old Factory, and two or three other places near here."

"Most of them places Johnny know," the young Indian said modestly. "Hunt seals – white whales – geese, them places."

"Then you will help us?"

For answer Johnny got to his feet.

"Not know Bay good like Charlie Eneveloe. No pilot so good like Charlie."

"That's all right. We've been to some of these places several times. We can help you." Jay turned to Ron. "This is an answer to prayer. Johnny has been on the government boat, so he's learned something about the channels and harbors, and he's hunted the mouths of the rivers and around the places where we have to go."

They waited while the Indian got his clothes and walked down to the *Good News* with him.

"That wind's beginning to whip up," Ron Orlis said, noting the way it swayed the tops of the scrubby trees. "Think we should go out in it?"

Jay thought for a moment.

"I'd like to get out of here if we can," he said, "just in case Peter Hoonah tries something else."

"I don't suppose the wind's blowing too strong for us to go out." Ron turned to Johnny. "Are there any other harbors close by where we can anchor if the storm does get too bad?"

"Many places. Each island two – three places."

"Good." Jay exclaimed. "I think we'd be better off anchored somewhere else than we would in staying here."

The tide was still high when they went aboard and started the engine.

"I can't say that I'm too keen about getting out there with the wind coming up the way it looks to be," Frank Thomas said as he and Ron cast off the lines and the *Good News* moved away from the pier, "but it's the only thing to do. We've got to get out of here."

Half the distance downstream toward the mouth of the river was smooth and effortless, but as they rounded the bend to head out to sea the waves began to build. They were huge, broad-beamed rollers that set the schooner to pitching. The waves were still smooth and dark, but it would not be long until they were wearing white crests as the increasing wind piled them high until the leading edge broke and curled over.

Ron Orlis turned the wheel to Johnny Goheen to take the *Good News* past the rocks that lined either side of the channel that led out to the open sea.

Frank Thomas came up to Ron.

"It's not as bad out here as I thought it would be," the Orlis boy said.

Concern still gleamed in Frank's eyes.

"I'll feel better when we get out into open water."

"What's the matter, Frank?" the young skipper said, "don't you trust Johnny's ability to pilot us?"

"I trust him all right, but–" For a moment he stood there in silence, looking out over the wind-swept Bay. "I was just talking with him a little while ago. He was on the government boat all right, but just as a deckhand. I don't think he even took the wheel once in his entire time with them. And, while he's seen the mouths of these rivers and knows where some of the harbors are, he still hasn't been into them in a boat the size of this. I'm not sure what ability he has as a pilot. He means well, but–"

The words choked in his throat.

At that very instant the engine of the *Good News* sputtered and died!

CHAPTER 9

JOHNNY GOHEEN'S DECISION

The *Good News* shuddered to a stop. The wind caught the bow and swung her half around. She wallowed heavily in the trough of one wave before being raised and swept shoreward by the next.

"The anchor!" Ron shouted above the wind. "Throw out the anchor!"

They sprang to it. And not an instant too soon. The *Good News* was being swept back toward the heavy granite boulders that lay along the rim of the channel. The anchor touched bottom and the hapless schooner turned slowly into the wind.

Ron Orlis dashed to the engine. Jay Russell was already there.

"What's the matter?" he demanded excitedly. "It's been running perfectly all the time."

"It sounded to me as though it's not getting gas."

"But that can't be. We checked the tanks this morning and filled them both."

"There could be something in the carburetor or plugging one of the gas lines."

"Whatever it is, we've got to find it and get under way fast. That anchor isn't going to hold us completely. I'm afraid the wind's going to take us back on the rocks."

Frank and Johnny Goheen joined them and hastily they began to take the carburetor apart. Tip and Eddie Skeena watched for a moment or two.

"Anything we can do to help?" the missionary's son asked.

"Just stay out of the way," his dad muttered, "that's all."

Tip backed away.

"What do you suppose would make the engine quit like that, Eddie?" he asked.

"Peter Hoonah." The Indian boy's eyes were wide with fright and his lips were trembling. "He do it. Now we all be killed because evil spirits much angry."

"The medicine man had something to do with it, all right," Tip admitted, "but I don't think the evil spirits did. I think he did it all himself."

"But how could that be? Your dad watch – Ron watch." Eddie shrugged his shoulders expressively. "Nobody come aboard." Conviction firmed his voice. "No sir, the evil spirits stop engine."

The missionary's son thought for a moment. "Nobody came aboard after we went to bed, that's true," he said.

"But that doesn't mean too much. We were all in the service for an hour. Hoonah had plenty of time to sneak aboard and do anything he wanted to."

Eddie remained unconvinced.

"Come on," Tip said, "let's look around and see what we can find."

The wind was rising and the *Good News* was pulling her anchor a little each time she pitched and rolled.

"We've got to get this engine fixed and right away," Ron Orlis muttered more to himself than to anyone else.

Tip started up on deck.

"Better not go up there, Tip!" his dad called to him. "You might have a rough time on deck. You could be washed overboard."

"O.K., Dad." Tip turned toward the stern. "Let's go back here, Eddie."

"What're you going to do?"

"Look around a little, that's all." Tip lowered his voice. "I was going to start up on deck, but I don't guess anything would have stayed on very long, the way we're pitching and rolling."

"What're we looking for?"

"Anything that we can find. I think old Peter Hoonah was on board."

Eddie shook his head vigorously but went with Tip.

Ron and Jay Russell finished putting the carburetor together and tried to start it.

"Oh God," Ron prayed under his breath. "Help it to start."

But nothing happened.

Ron Orlis looked out at the heavy, pounding seas. They were moving! Not much but a little as each powerful wave dragged the anchor a foot or two.

"Dear God!" A wordless cry for help went up from his heart. Icy fingers grasped his chest and squeezed the breath from his lungs.

"Ron," Tip said, coming up to him. "What's this?"

"Don't bother me right now, Tip," he said. "We've got to trace down the reason our engine's not getting any gas, or it'll be too late."

There was a brief silence.

"Ron–" Tip said.

But the Orlis boy had already turned back to the engine.

"Ron–"

"Come on," Eddie Skeena said, disgust edging his voice. "I know that thing didn't come off Peter Hoonah's clothes."

"But I know it did," Tip persisted. "I saw it fastened on him somewhere."

At the mention of Peter Hoonah, Ron turned quickly. "What have you got that you think belongs to that old rascal?"

He stared at the beaded moosehide tassel Tip held in his hand.

"That is from Peter Hoonah's clothes," he exclaimed. "Where did you find it?"

"Right back here," Tip said. "At the corner of this box."

"The old medicine man was here last night," Jay Russell said. "He's the one who's responsible for this!"

He straightened quickly.

"But what could he – I've got it!" He lunged back to the rear of the engine, pushed a box of supplies aside and fumbled with the valve. "I thought I'd found the trouble." Dismay flooded his voice. "But I didn't. The valve was on."

Ron Orlis bent down and examined the valve.

"What're you looking for?" Jay asked.

"Get me a wrench, will you, Jay?"

"What is it?"

"Old Hoonah was too clever to turn off the valve. He must have figured we'd find that. But he did think he'd fool us by putting something into the gas line to clog it."

Jay handed him the wrench. "How do you know all of that so suddenly?"

"There are plier marks on the copper nut on this fitting," Ron worked as he talked. In an instant the fitting was loose.

"Just as I thought!" He held up a short piece of sinew that had been shoved into the gas line. "Now try it!"

The engine sputtered once or twice and took hold with a welcoming roar.

"Thank God!" Ron breathed prayerfully.

Ron Orlis and Johnny Goheen made their way up to the wheelhouse while Frank Thomas and Jay Russell plunged forward along the pitching deck to lift the anchor. Slowly the *Good News* began to inch forward.

The young American expelled a sigh of relief. "I didn't think we were ever going to make it out of here," he said.

"Neither did I."

Ron noticed the odd, pinched tone in the new pilot's voice. "I thought maybe old Peter Hoonah had turned the evil spirits loose on us."

He laughed as he spoke, but Ron saw that he was serious.

"You know, Johnny," the Orlis boy said, "we have nothing to fear from evil spirits. Ours is a powerful God."

The young Indian nodded his agreement. "I see He is powerful enough to keep Peter Hoonah from hurting us."

"He not only is powerful enough to keep Peter Hoonah from hurting us," Ron said, speaking slowly and carefully. "He is powerful enough to save us from the results of our sin."

Johnny thought about that for two or three minutes while the *Good News* lifted high on one wave to plunge down the other side and burrow its stubby bow in the crest of the next. It came up slowly, shaking off the spray, to repeat the process.

"You mean He can save Johnny Goheen from sin?"

"He saved me from sin. He can save you," Ron went on. "The Bible says, 'all have sinned and fall short of the glory of God.' That means that no one has ever lived the way he should except the Lord Jesus Christ. 'But the free gift of God is eternal life in Christ Jesus our Lord.' If we know that we are sinners and put our trust in the Lord Jesus Christ to save us, He will."

Johnny took a deep breath.

"If Robert had died when he was in the water, he wouldn't have gone to heaven, would he?"

"Does he know the Lord Jesus Christ as his personal Savior?"

The pilot shook his head. "He, like me, he not know about Jesus."

"The Bible says that confessing your sin and putting your trust in the Lord Jesus Christ for salvation is the only way you can be saved. According to that, Robert would not have gone to heaven." He paused and glanced at Johnny. "But just think how gracious God is. He spared Robert's life so he will have a chance to take Christ as his Savior."

Johnny ran a trembling hand over his forehead and wiped away the sweat.

"Don't you think you should take Christ as your Savior?" the Orlis boy persisted.

Johnny Goheen's nod was almost imperceptible.

There in the wheelhouse with the *Good News* bucking and plunging over the waves, the youthful Indian asked God to forgive him and to come into his heart.

A feeling of joy took hold of Ron that he had seldom known before. In that moment he thanked God wordlessly for calling him to the North as his full-time Christian service. As soon as he got out of Bible school and could get his support, he would be living in a place like this working with this same kind of people. *They would be his people.*

But that was wrong. *They were already his people,*

An hour later the little schooner had made its way out of the channel and was angling southwest, keeping the stubby prow quartered into the wind.

Jay Russell came into the wheelhouse.

"What do you think, Ron? Should we put up for the night?"

"I thought it would probably be best if we did. There's no place for us to get in out of the wind there if it should keep on blowing."

"I'm afraid it's going to keep on blowing, all right," the missionary observed. "It looks to me as though we're in for a few days of it."

They talked with Johnny Goheen, consulted a map, and decided on a little cove on the lee side of an island away from the wind. Johnny, it developed, knew the Bay a little better than Frank Thomas thought he did. He guided the *Good News* between the islands, probing out a narrow channel, and coming to a stop in the still water behind the island.

"Well, we made it," Ron said triumphantly. "Let 'er blow."

"You weren't saying that a few hours ago," the missionary told him, laughing.

"And neither was anyone else."

They were all in good spirits after getting in out

of the wind and were joking and laughing about anything. At last Ron grew serious. He turned to Eddie Skeena, the young stowaway. "Still want to go to Fort George?" he asked.

The boy nodded.

"I was just thinking, Eddie. There's no need in our hauling all the lumber to Paint Hills first. We'll take the next load to Fort George."

The boy's eyes lit up, although he made no comment.

"And to show you that I'm a good friend of yours I'm going to let you come down and help me with dinner."

Eddie followed Ron down into the galley.

"What we going have, Ron?" he asked.

"Get out some flour and we'll make some bannock first. Then I'll see what cans we have to open."

The Indian boy opened the flour barrel.

His face twisted and he put his finger into it and tasted it.

"Oooh, that's terrible! Ron, come here a minute, will you?"

"What's the trouble? Don't tell me that we're out of flour."

"No, there's plenty of it, but I don't know who could eat it. It tastes and smells awful."

Ron Orlis sniffed.

"Kerosene!"

CHAPTER 10

ANOTHER DECISION

"But who would put kerosene in our flour?" Eddie Skeena asked,

"I'll give you three guesses," Ron retorted darkly, "and you won't have to use two of them."

"P-Peter Hoonah?"

"Peter Hoonah. He was a busy little man when he got aboard last night during the service."

"What are we going to do now?"

"That's a good question. We left most of our supplies at Thompson, thinking we'd be able to pick up more at Paint Hills."

He straightened and looked out the porthole at the trees on top of the island's only hill that were bending and swaying in the wind.

"And," he concluded forebodingly, "it looks as though we'll be here for a few days – maybe a week."

He started for the door.

"Well, come on, Eddie, let's go up and break the bad news to Tip and the others."

"Peter Hoonah sure wasn't taking any chances with us, was he?" Frank Thomas put in. "He was going to drown us by getting us smashed on the rocks when our motor quit, and if that didn't work, he was going to starve us to death." "There should be enough food down there to last us for a little while," Ron said. "Come on. Let's go down and see what he left us."

They went down to the galley and took a quick inventory of their stores. Hoonah had ruined the flour and must have thrown their lard overboard or stolen it. At least it was gone. Only a little canned goods was left, and even there, he had torn the labels off.

"It doesn't look as though we've got as much food as we thought we had," Jay Russell said. "Think we can make it last?"

"That depends." Ron squinted up at the swaying trees once more. "How long is the wind going to blow?"

"It could blow for two or three days," Johnny said, "or twice that long."

Jay Russell grinned.

"It won't be the first time I've had to tighten my belt. I guess it won't hurt me to do it again."

Ron Orlis broke out a box of crackers, doled them out four to each person, and made a pot of tea. At the table, quite suddenly, Johnny Goheen gave his testimony.

"You spoke Jesus to me," he said, "I see you stand up to Peter Hoonah when everyone else scared to. I know you have something I don't. I–I think I would become Christian first night I hear Frank preach, but I–I not understand."

His face broke into a big smile.

"Now I understand," he said.

"I'm still hungry," Tip Russell said, getting up from the table to turn in for the night.

"We'll go out and see if we can get some berries tomorrow," his dad said. "There should be a lot of berries around at this time of the year."

"Pick berries?" the missionary's son echoed, wrinkling his nose. "Who wants to pick berries?"

"I'll admit they don't sound too good when a fellow is thinking about a nice juicy piece of roast beef," his dad said, "but when you're hungry, berries can look awfully good to you."

"Not good enough so I'll want to pick 'em," Tip said. "I can tell you that much."

"If a fellow doesn't pick berries and we go berry picking," Jay Russell countered, "he won't eat."

"Then I just won't eat," Tip retorted quickly.

The following morning, they decided upon eating two meals a day until the wind went down so they could get out.

"What should we do about getting some more food?" Ron asked. "Do you suppose there's anything besides berries on these islands?"

"There be ducks," Johnny said. "Most islands have ducks. We might be able get rabbits if we have bullets."

"We don't have much," Jay put in. "Not over four or five rounds."

"If we wait until we get a good shot each time, we should be able to do all right," Ron Orlis said.

"And, of course, we can fish," Frank said.

"What do we go after first?" Ron asked.

"I vote for berries," Frank spoke up. "We can scout around for game and be sure of getting something to eat at the same time."

They found various containers to put their berries in and started for the deck.

"Tip," Eddie said, "aren't you coming?"

"Nope. I said that I don't pick berries. Especially those that are half green like they'll be this time of year."

"They'll be something for us to eat. Aren't you hungry?" the Indian boy asked. "You heard what they said about not getting to eat if you didn't pick berries."

"I heard them, but I'm not that hungry. Besides, I'm going to fish in a little while and get something good to eat."

Tip thought the Indian boy would stay with him, but he was the first one into the lifeboat when they got it in the water.

"You can suit yourself, Tip," his dad countered, "but what we said still goes. Anyone who doesn't help with getting the food isn't going to get to eat."

"I'll get something to eat, Dad. Don't worry about that."

"They all left the *Good News* and a few minutes later the missionary's son saw them head up the hill on the near side of the island.

Tip watched them go. When they were out of sight, he got out the fishing tackle and began to fish off deck. Fishing wasn't too good at this time of year, and he had the added handicap of being without a small boat to get around in. Still, he should be able to get something before the fellows got back. He just had to.

An hour passed before he got his first bite. He felt the tremor on the rod and tightened his grip. Hopefully, he struck, but the fish was gone. For an instant disappointment welled within him. Still, it was encouraging to have a bite. That meant there were fish around.

"Sooner or later, I'll get one," he told himself.

However, minutes dragged into an hour, and then two hours, and there was not another hint of activity on his line.

He glanced uneasily up the hill. In another hour or so the fellows would be coming back. He had to get something. He just had to.

That was when he saw the ducks. His lithe young body tensed, and his eyes went wide and staring. Ducks! Three of them! A huge mallard drake and two smaller hens. Where they had come from, he didn't know. Perhaps they had been there all the time. But that didn't matter. They were swimming placidly along, almost within range.

They were getting closer. Tip watched momentarily, not even daring to breathe. All thought of getting meat to show the others was gone. He had to get those ducks. He just had to. Hurriedly he crept down to the cabin where the rifle was kept, got the ammunition and slipped it in the chamber.

When he got back, he didn't see the ducks for an instant and his heart faltered. There they were, swimming slowly away from the boat! They were still too far away. Numbly he raised his rifle to his shoulder and waited.

After what seemed to be an hour or two, but was probably only that many minutes, the ducks turned and began to make their way back. They were getting closer. They loomed large in the scope. He just might be able to hit them, but it would be better to let them get as close as they would. If they turned again and started away, he–

Tip Russell was about to squeeze the trigger when he heard a queer barking noise behind him.

A seal!

He turned quickly. There it was sunning on a big rock ledge. A half-grown hair seal – enough meat for everyone for a week. Not very good meat, but it was meat. A prayer on his lips, he jerked the rifle around and fired.

A shudder went through the seal's body. He hit him! He hit him!

The seal raised himself on his front fins and Tip's exultation died within him. His bullet hadn't struck a vital spot. The seal would be heading for the sea!

Tip shot again. The seal staggered forward. Hurriedly, he fired a third time and a fourth. The seal dropped on the edge of the rock and for a tantalizing instant or two lay there, quivering. Tip watched helplessly as he gave a final spasmodic jerk and toppled into the water!

A groan of anguish escaped the boy's lips.

When the berry picking party came back with only a few berries for their efforts, Tip was sitting dejectedly on the edge of his bunk, his chin buried in his hand.

"I hope you had better luck fishing than we had berry picking, Tip," Ron told him.

No answer.

"Where are those fish you were going to catch for us?"

Deliberately Tip Russell forced himself to look straight into Ron's eyes.

"Ron," he said miserably, "I really loused things up."

By this time, the others were standing there, listening in silence.

"What'd you do?" the Orlis boy asked, "throw our fishing tackle overboard?"

"Worse than that. I shot up all our ammunition and didn't get a thing."

Hesitantly he told them all that had happened.

"I–I'm sorry I didn't go with you fellows," he stammered, "and I–I'm sorry I didn't leave the gun alone. I knew we only had four bullets and that I don't shoot well enough to have risked it. Now I've put everybody in a mess."

Jay Russell spoke quietly.

"This is the sort of thing that happens when we disobey," he said.

Nobody mentioned the matter to Tip again, but the group was unusually quiet that evening. After devotions Ron Orlis got the fishing gear and went up on deck to fish. Then, Eddie Skeena came up and stood beside him.

"Catch anything?"

"Not yet."

"Not very good place for fishing."

"That's for sure." Ron shifted his rod to the other hand. "I thought I'd take the lifeboat and go out for a while in the morning if the wind's still up."

Eddie's homely young face was solemn.

"Isn't anybody mad at Tip?"

Ron turned to face him quizzically.

"What do you mean?"

"For what he did. Now we all go hungry."

"Tip knows that what he did was wrong. I don't think he will ever do it again."

That didn't seem to satisfy Eddie.

"But we all go hungry," he persisted. "And you nice to him. Me – much mad!" His young eyes flashed their hostility.

"Tip told us that he's sorry, and we said we'd forgive him. We can't stay angry with him because of what he did any more than for God to stay angry with us after He has forgiven us our sin."

Eddie thought about that for a time.

"You mean if I – if person confess his sin to God and accept Jesus as his Savior, God not be angry any more for what we have do?"

"That's right."

"Just like you and Frank and Johnny not angry at Tip for what he do?"

"It's a little different than that," Ron said, searching for words to explain. "We're human, so when we get good and hungry, we're apt to start thinking about what Tip did, even though we told him we would forgive him. We may have to pray and ask God to help us not to hold what happened against him. But when God forgives, He wipes the sin out. It's gone like the winter snows when the summer sun comes."

Eddie stood beside Ron for a long while, his eyes fastened fixedly on the water. Then, still without saying a word, he turned and walked away.

It was half an hour later that he came back.

"Ron." His voice was soft but charged with emotion. "Can I talk to you?"

"Sure." Ron reeled in his line. "I was just going to quit fishing anyway."

He sat down and leaned against the rail.

"What's on your mind, Eddie."

The boy cleared his throat and swallowed hard.

"I–I–Do you think God forgive me?" he blurted.

"Of course, God will forgive you," Ron said, "providing you meet His conditions."

"What you mean, 'conditions'?"

"First of all, you've got to really be sorry for the things you've done that are bad, Eddie. Not just sorry someone found out about it, but really sorry you ever did it – sorry that you even thought about doing it.

"Then you've got to know that you are lost, that if you would die now – this very evening – you would not go to heaven, you would go to hell. Then you've got to believe that the Lord Jesus Christ can save you and that He will save you." Ron paused, eyeing the boy carefully to be sure he understood. "When you do those things, you have met God's conditions and He will forgive you for sin."

Eddie weighed the matter in his mind.

"If–if I do those things, then I be Christian?"

"That's right, Eddie. If you do those things, you'll be a Christian."

"My father, he medicine man like Peter Hoonah," he said, his voice numb. "If I am Christian, he get angry. Much angry."

"It wouldn't be easy for you," Ron admitted. "I wouldn't say that it would. It might be terribly hard. But, of course, it wasn't easy for Christ on the cross, either. And, He was dying for our sin, not His own, because He did not sin."

Eddie said no more to Ron that evening, but the following morning he came to the galley where Ron was boiling water for tea.

"Ron," the Indian lad said seriously. "I do it."

At first the Orlis boy did not understand.

"What?"

"I do it," he said simply. "Last night after I leave you, I think what you say. I want to be Christian, so I wake up Tip and talk to him. He help me pray."

"That's wonderful, Eddie! I'm so happy for you."

Johnny Goheen came into the galley just then.

"Have you heard the news?" he asked excitedly. "The wind's going down."

"Have you heard Eddie's news?" Ron asked.

Questions leaped to Johnny's eyes.

"News?"

The Indian boy gulped.

"I same as you, Johnny," he said, fumbling for words. "I Christian now."

The older Indian lad came over and sat down.

"That is good news, Eddie. You not be sorry."

Jay Russell stuck his head in the galley.

"You'd better hurry with that tea, Ron," he said. "The wind's going down and the tide's beginning to go out. We'll have to get under way."

Ron Orlis turned off the burner. "We can always make tea," he said. "Right now, I think we'd better get out to sea."

They lifted the anchor and Johnny took the helm to guide the *Good News* out into open water once more. The waves were still running high, but the wind had eased noticeably, and the white caps were no longer showing.

Eddie came into the wheelhouse with Ron and the pilot after a time.

"So, you are Christian now," Johnny said, his eyes and voice smiling.

"Yes, I am Christian," the boy answered, "only it not be so easy, maybe. My father, he get much mad. Like Peter Hoonah…He medicine man."

Johnny's eyes narrowed. "You are going to tell him?"

"What else can I do?" he asked simply. "He have to know that I no longer follow old ways."

"I go with you," Johnny Goheen said firmly. "When we get to Fort George, I go with you to talk to your father. We tell him about Jesus."

"You will?" Eddie's eyes lit gratefully.

"And we pray about it that he make Christian, too, O.K.?"

Ron Orlis listened to them, his heart rejoicing. He had come to James Bay to run a boat and haul lumber, but God had given him the joy of having a part in dealing with two precious souls. The rest of the work would go well now. He was sure of that.

He stood and looked out across the sparkling water.

How anxious he was to finish school so he could get up in the North and work among the people God was giving him.

THE DANNY ORLIS SERIES

The Danny Orlis series, by Bernard Palmer, delivers a blend of adventure, mystery, and suspense through various settings—from the Canadian wilderness to Guatemalan jungles. Danny Orlis, an adept outdoorsman, skilled athlete, and committed Christian, employs his quick thinking, calm bravery, and biblical solutions to confront everyday problems and hair-raising dangers. Early stories focus on Danny navigating school life, sports, and outdoor challenges, while in later books, Danny and his wife Kay provide wisdom and guidance to youngsters facing lifelike situations and challenges. Having sold over two million copies, this series has made Palmer a renowned author in Christian youth literature. Palmer is also the author of the Felicia Cartright series and various other series for Christian youth.

AVAILABLE FROM WWW.ANEKOPRESS.COM

www.ingramcontent.com/pod-product-compliance
Lightning Source LLC
Chambersburg PA
CBHW060505300726
48975CB00008B/2649